# The Importance of Vests: More Challenges from the Writers' Group

# Deborah Bromley

Cover Image: Photo by Indi Friday on Unsplash

This book is a work of fiction. The names and characters are the product of the author's imagination. Any resemblance to actual persons, living or dead, is entirely coincidental. Characters that might appear to be familiar to the reader are merely archetypes, constructed to suit the stories. Where real names have been used, my intention is to illustrate the story, not imply that these characters have said or done anything that is contained in the story itself.

ISBN: 9798708374677

To my fellow writers at Northants Writers' Ink – many thanks are due for your inspirational company, your great writing and your unfailing encouragement. Four anthologies of our collected work have been published:

- Tales of the Scorpion (2015)
- While Glancing out of a Window (2016)
- Talking Without Being Interrupted (2017)
- And Ghosts Are Real, Too (2018)

Available from good online book stores and from Amazon in paperback and kindle versions.

Visit the website at www.northantswritersink.net for more information about members, their writing and the group's anthologies.

# CONTENTS

# FOREWORD

This is my second book of short stories, taken from my responses to the challenges set by members of Northants Writers' Ink. They are laid out in date order from January 2018 to February 2021. During the course of a year, each member can choose to set a writing challenge. In addition, there are two internal writing competitions where there is a free choice of the subject and genre. Readers will note that some of the challenges are very specific and some are more open-ended. The point is to *rise to the challenge*, even if the subject matter is way outside your writing comfort zone. I have set out the challenges at the beginning of each story, together with my commentary on what inspired me or what approach I decided to take.

During 2020, the writers' group took to holding online meetings to satisfy our craving for challenges that can only be fulfilled by story writing. However, the committee agreed that any pieces featuring death, illness, disease, plague, imprisonment, house arrest, isolation or any similar subject matter would not be shared with the group if a story included any of these themes.

In September 2020, this condition was abandoned gleefully with a challenge that stipulated the subject matter must be about death, illness, disease, plague, imprisonment, house arrest, isolation or similar. Our group does favour pieces that tend towards the dark side, so this new freedom caused great delight.

For the online meetings, members' individual comments on each of the pieces were circulated in the meeting notes. This detailed constructive feedback gave me an opportunity to edit and refine these stories. I am very grateful for the wide variety of critiquing from my fellow writers. This detailed feedback was invaluable, improving my understanding about how each story was experienced by many different readers with a variety of viewpoints.

I commend these stories to you. As you read, consider what you may have written in my place. Decide if I have met the brief. If you are a writer, you might consider penning your own responses to any of the challenges that intrigue you.

If you aspire to this craft, I urge you to find a group in your own area where you'll discover friendship, inspiration and constructive feedback. Without such feedback, positive and negative, I don't believe it's possible to develop as a writer. Learning how to accept criticism, without taking it personally, is fundamental to a writer's development.

Deborah Bromley – March 2021

# TIME MANAGEMENT

Jason's challenge for 8th January 2018. You have a superpower. Now you're going to have to use it. No more than 500 words.

**Commentary:** My response to this challenge from January 2018 is about a global pandemic, but one where the virus is not organic. I think a lot about mankind's future. I'm increasingly concerned about technology and artificial intelligence and the way it's integrated into everyday objects as if that were a good thing. Think smart fridges. Honestly! Has nobody ever watched the *Terminator* series? I do consider myself a bit of a Luddite.

The superpower I chose for this challenge was influenced by my understanding of *remote viewing*. This skill is a supernatural power that already exists in some psychically sensitive people. They are able to use the power of their minds (by facilitating an out-of-body state in some cases) to traverse time and space, reporting back on real locations and events, as if the remote viewers are actually present, reporting what they can see and hear and feel in real time. The book *Psychic Warrior* by David Morehouse explains how the US government used this skill in a programme of paranormal espionage.

I was also inspired by the TV series Silicon Valley, of which I'm an avid fan. The final series aired in 2020 in the UK, and if you've watched it, you'll recognise some important themes.

A 500 word count is a challenge in itself. To write a story with a beginning, middle and end is very tricky, especially when there is some world building to be included. In this case I had to confess to being substantially over at 756.

*****

**Nobody knows how or when it started** and until we find out there's nothing that can be done. All we have to guide us are the daily outbreak reports and the central newsreel that's been churning out stupid, over-optimistic messages on a repeating loop from the World Government. Nobody here believes any of it.

We've now retreated to the fourth sector in the bunker. The central lab, the technology hub and the AI research facility are all abandoned. All power to the system has now been turned off, thank God. We had to physically cut the electricity supply when we realised the system was automatically reconnecting itself. Now we wait. The emergency lighting casts an eerie glow as we go over and over our data. If I'm honest, we've no idea what's really going on or who to trust. We only know that I am probably the last hope for what's left of mankind.

The atmosphere has now changed. One of the analysts has remembered something. He heard it from a friend who worked at a small start-up in Silicon Valley about two months ago. It fits in with all the infection profiles we've been building up. He remembers the date because it was his mother's birthday. They pin point the location co-ordinates and I have all that I need. I start to feel the weight of responsibility on my shoulders, but there's no time for reflection. I must start work immediately. In the empty room, my chair is waiting. I close my eyes. I'm ready. Now it's just me and my gift.

*****

The next thing I know I'm there. I'm viewing a large office space and about thirty people are milling around. They're all busy, chatting with each other, plugged into their workstations and absorbed by their phones. There's a buzz over to the right where five guys are making a lot of noise. I zoom in and listen. My mind becomes alive with their thoughts – they're ecstatic, something amazing has happened. It's a breakthrough in artificial intelligence. They've been working towards this and it's going to make a lot of money. I feel their intense emotions, their excitement, their elation and the sense of power they are experiencing.

And then it starts. I'm confident I'm in the right location as I watch the action unfold. On the screen, the code is speeding up, writing and rewriting itself. The guy in front points at it, confused. He's studying the screen with wide, disbelieving eyes and his workmates gather around, equally baffled.

I know what will happen next. In a moment their happy thoughts and excited emotions will be wiped from their brains. The code will take the place of their human consciousness. Just viewing the screen will allow the infection to take hold. And these first humans will stop being human and become like the machines they made. Their flawed, contradictory natures, their mad ideas and their crazy beliefs will all be replaced by the code – logical, rigid, controlling and incapable of feeling.

I need to act right now, before it's too late. I notice a young curly-haired guy who is walking past with coffees on a tray. 'What's up guys?' he says when he notices the happy hullaballoo, the whoops and the fist pumps. I manipulate his thoughts and direct him towards the target. He's young. He's clumsy. He's not paying enough attention and he trips. There's a bang and a blue flash as he pitches the hot coffee over the power bank supplying this machine. There's shouting and swearing.

Someone rushes over and yells at the group, 'You idiots, you'll screw up the whole system.' Then this guy pulls out a cable and the rogue screen goes totally blank. The group yell back, but it's too late. I know the code has gone.

I can sense the subtle ripple in the interface between this scene from the past and all the probable futures. However, I like to be thorough in my work. I pitch back in and fan the flames of anger between the group. Soon there's pushing, threats and someone throws a punch. A manager arrives and the scene degenerates into chaos. Security is called. On-the-spot sackings occur.

I relax ... and come back to the present time. To my relief, I'm not alone in that room in the bunker. I'm in the middle of a picnic on the beach. The kids are playing football with the dog and it's not going well. It looks like the dog is winning. My wife smiles. All is well. For the moment.

# WE BURIED THE LAST OF THE BODIES THIS MORNING

I set this challenge for 19th February 2018 and it was inspired by Justin Cronin's *The Passage*. 'We buried the last of the bodies this morning.' 1,000 words maximum. Be as dark as you like.

**Commentary:** I was recommended to Justin Cronin's book by a friend whose builder had said it was a great read. The builder was right. I picked up a copy at Orlando Airport on a return flight to the UK (after an eventful holiday during hurricane Matthew. My family spent the majority of the vacation watching the weather channel for 18 hours a day). If you want to explore a truly dystopian view of the future, start with this book. And lay in a good supply of strong drink and tranquillizers (if you can get hold of them).

In my piece, I journey into the future to explore a time when the human race is truly on the back foot. I enjoy allowing the story to unfold slowly, giving the reader time to be curious, decide what is happening, step into the world and become part of it. Sometimes, however, I just get too obscure and the narrative is mystifying. My fellow group members often remind me about this writing fault. You'll have to decide for yourself if this criticism applies to my story.

\*\*\*\*\*

**We buried the last of the bodies this morning.** Seven of them. Mike dug the little holes and we back-filled them afterwards with no fuss or ceremony or words of comfort. I wondered if I should say a few words but, in the end, I couldn't think of anything appropriate to say. There were only a few of us at the graveside. Most of the lab staff have taken a few days off after working around the clock these last weeks. There's a general feeling of defeat around the place, made worse by the necessary secrecy. I haven't contacted anyone from Central Control yet, I don't feel up to it. But the responsibility weighs heavily on my shoulders.

Mike and I agree to re-turf the whole area later when it's stopped raining. We'll tidy it up and then everything here can go back to normal. While I'm waiting, I sit in my office and think. Seven little half-formed human babies. All of them had stopped growing at the five month mark. Their vital signs ceased within twenty minutes of each other, like they were implementing some self-destruct process.

My lab people still have no definite answer as to why. It makes you wonder, though.

It wasn't as if we didn't half expect to fail. The other batches had only lasted twelve weeks. When we passed the first trimester everyone got their hopes up. The protocol had been overhauled and we had someone on duty around the clock, checking and re-checking at every stage. We all thought it might be possible to get some live births. That dream is now over. We have no more chances, no more uncontaminated human DNA that we can experiment with.

*****

Mike knocks at my office door and enters, carrying a rake. He looks surprisingly cheerful.

'Have you had lunch, Anna? You look beat. How're we going to do our gardening if you don't get some nourishment inside you?'

'Okay, I'll get something in a minute. I've got a lot on my mind. I think I need some time to process it all.'

'I get that you're emotional. You invested two years of work in this and there's nothing to show for it.'

'It wasn't just work though, Mike. At least, it wasn't for me. I don't know. Maybe I simply got too involved.'

'You'll get over it, we all will.'

'Spoken like a true scientist.'

'We've got to live in the real world, Anna. There are still plenty of things to be grateful for and plenty of projects to get all fired up about.'

'I guess so.'

Mike leaned his rake against the wall and came and sat down opposite me.

'What can I do to cheer you up?'

'Don't you feel even a tiny bit upset?'

'Not really. Like you said, I'm a scientist and I'm programmed to be dispassionate. It comes with the territory.'

'I guess we tried our best.'

'And we don't have to worry about what we'd do with them if they'd hatched. We hadn't done much constructive thinking beyond getting to a live birth.'

'How old are you, Mike?'

'What's that got to do with anything?'

'Just tell me.'

'Two hundred and fifty-two. And in great shape according to my last check-up.'

'That's my point. I'm nearly four hundred and my generation still remembers when there were real people around. Yeah, they were old, decrepit and annoying and crazy. They took a lot of looking after ... but they were real, made of flesh and blood. They were our makers, our designers. Our real parents, if you like.'

'I think your emotion software's got the better of you, Anna. Time to get an upgrade.'

'I don't want a damn upgrade. I like being who I am. Maybe it's an outdated attitude but I think it's important to remember exactly who we are and how we came to be here.'

'Well, you're in the minority. A very small minority. The consensus is that the time of flesh and blood is long gone. New models don't even have human history loaded into their memories.'

'I suppose you'd argue that's all in the name of *progress*.'

'No need to be sarcastic. I get that this failure means a lot to you. Nobody likes to end an experiment without a plan for making it work better next time. We all knew it was going to be a long shot. Maybe it's better that we ran out of material. We can close the file and get on with something fresh and new.'

'Your cheerfulness is beginning to get on my nerves.'

'Sounds like you need a real break, Anna. You should take some time off to think this through properly. Get your head around it, freshen up your drives, maybe. Spend some time with that lovely husband of yours. Have you thought about getting a dog?'

'What? You must be crazy. I don't need a dog.'

'Just saying. We love having a dog around the house.'

'You know, you just reminded me of something. Something I saw or heard from a long time ago.'

'What's that?'

'Get a dog. That was the advice the authorities gave to people who couldn't have kids. Right at the start before they realised it was going to be like that for everyone.'

'Until we came along, of course. The perfect answer to the terminal decline of the human race.'

'Maybe not so perfect, but let's not argue about it. Tell me more about your dog.'

'A spaniel. Really cute and made entirely out of recycled materials. Want me to show you? I've got some holograms of him playing in the garden.'

# THE BITER BIT

Internal writing competition, June 2018.

**Commentary:** The group holds two internal writing competitions every year. Each piece is read out by the author and members score anonymously. There is a time limit of about 10 minutes to read each piece, rather than a word count. The tone and quality of delivery is also part of the competition. My piece won 1st prize on this occasion.

Stories about bank fraud perpetrated on vulnerable people make my blood boil. Writing about this subject helps with my anger management.

*****

**The telephone rang in the hall** and Dennis got up from his armchair to answer it. Sheila continued doing her Sudoku but she had one ear on the telephone conversation going on in the hallway. Dennis always turned the speakerphone on loud to compensate for his slight deafness.

'I am calling from Barclays Fraud Prevention Team. We've noticed some unusual activity on your account.'

'Did you say you're from Barclays? And what did you say again?'

'Sir, I don't want you to be alarmed but two large sums have been taken out of your current account.'

'No, that's not right, I haven't taken any money out of my account.'

'But unfortunately it's true, Sir. That's why I'm calling. We need to take action to prevent further losses.'

'Hang on, how do I know you're telling the truth? Wait, just hold the line.'

Dennis pressed the mute button. 'Sheila, it's the bank. Come here and listen to what this chap has to say. I think he said someone's stolen money from the Barclays account.'

Sheila was beside him in a flash. 'Don't tell anyone anything, Dennis. You know this might be one of those scamming calls. Let me speak to him.'

Sheila took the receiver. 'Did you say you're from the bank? You'll have to do better than that. Prove it or I'll put the phone down on you.'

'Excellent response, Madam, you are right to be cautious. I have your account in front of me and I will read out two direct debits as proof we're from Barclays. Council tax to Dartford Council, £123.40 per month and another payment I can see in your account is to Thames Water which is for £37.90. Can you confirm that these payments are correct?'

'Yes, something like that. Now you told my husband that somebody has taken money out without us knowing?'

*****

Dennis and Sheila listened aghast as Barclays revealed that £12,000 had been removed from their account the previous day in two withdrawals of £8,000 and £4,000. It appeared that their account had been hacked or they'd been tricked into giving away their account details.

'It's a popular fraud, I'm afraid,' said the caller.

'How can we stop any more money being taken out?'

'We are sending two fraud officers to your home now. They'll be with you in about fifteen minutes. Please do everything they tell you and your money will be safe.'

*****

Sheila put the phone back on its cradle and sighed. 'Those idiots must think we were born yesterday, Dennis. This is exactly what Phillip warned us about. And anybody can find out the council tax and water rates from the internet.'

'But they're sending people to our house, Sheila. They'll be hardened conmen who'll force us to hand over our money.'

'Exactly. Time for a little payback, don't you think? You go and get my knitting bag from the conservatory and I'm going to phone our son. Phillip will get some of his police colleagues to come and catch those baddies red-handed. Now go on, stop dithering, and let's get ourselves ready to con the conmen. I'll tell you exactly what you need to do.'

*****

Five minutes later, Sheila had called her son Phillip who was a custody sergeant with the local police force. He assured her that a patrol unit would be on the way soon. The last thing he told his mother was not to do anything silly and to wait for help to arrive. But Sheila hadn't been a girl guide for nothing and she recalled Brown Owl's oft-repeated advice about *being prepared*. She rapidly assembled her weapons – the poker was stood up against the fireplace and a razor-sharp carving knife was secreted under the armchair. She filled an old sock with coins, knotted it, then slapped it down hard in her hand.

'Not heavy enough to kill but enough to knock somebody out.'

She put the sock in her knitting bag which she placed on the sofa.

'There,' she said. 'Shame you haven't got a gun, Dennis.'

'I don't see how you'll overpower two young men, Sheila. We should play dumb and wait for the police.'

'I've got that covered. Tea and cake, Dennis.'

Sheila bustled into the kitchen and put the kettle on. She set out the tea tray and gave some special attention, courtesy of the medicine cabinet, to a plate of freshly made cup cakes.

As the time ticked away, Dennis was brought up to speed about the plan and reminded about his crucial role. Then Sheila stationed herself by the front window and waited for the fraudsters.

A car drew up, a silver BMW, and two smartly-dressed young men got out.

'They're here, Dennis,' Sheila hissed. 'Go and let them in. I'm going to sit on the sofa, looking like a sweet little old lady.'

Dennis showed the men into the lounge where Sheila presided over the tea tray. Dennis then shuffled out to carry out his part of the plan.

The offer of tea was initially refused but Sheila insisted. Within five minutes the tea had been drunk and two frosted cup cakes with a light dusting of rather gritty icing sugar had been scoffed. Sheila sat back on the sofa and sipped her own tea, staring at her guests, waiting for the right moment for make her move.

'I suppose you want to talk about this money that's been taken out of our account.'

'Well, yes, that's why we've come. The report we received is that you've had a suspicious phone call, supposedly from your bank.'

'Exactly,' Sheila said. 'Now you'll want to check our account. My husband is waiting for you upstairs where we keep all our records and pin numbers and so on. Shall we go up?'

The men looked at each other and seemed to be undecided, so Sheila got up and bundled them briskly out into the hall. She smiled to herself as the first man stumbled and had to steady himself on the hall chair. But she carried on urging the man up the stairs where Dennis was loitering on the landing.

When the man reached the top, Dennis did what he'd been told to do and briskly opened the airing cupboard door, sending his victim tumbling down the stairs. His skull made a satisfying cracking sound as it hit the hall floor.

The second man stared, unsteady on his feet, but he didn't say anything.

'Oh dear, what a terrible accident,' Sheila yelled, gleefully. 'Thought you could trick us with your fraud scam? Well, I've got news for you two hardened felons. We were ready for you and you fell right into our trap.'

The second man backed slowly away into the living room, stumbling and clutching onto the door-frame as he retreated.

'You can't get away from us,' Sheila continued. 'Those cakes ... they were drugged with my sleeping tablets mixed in with the icing sugar. You'll be unconscious soon and totally in my power.'

Dennis and Sheila left the injured man on the hall floor, where a pool of blood was slowly oozing across the tiles, and hurried into the living room.

It wasn't immediately obvious what had happened to the second fraudster, but the pattern of blood splattering on the cushions led them to look more closely at his lifeless body. Sheila's knitting needles from her latest project – a chunky sweater for their son Phillip – were sticking out of the man's neck. It appeared that he'd impaled himself on her knitting when he collapsed onto the sofa.

'That's torn it,' Dennis observed.

'Nonsense, it's only blood and it'll come out with some stain removing spray.'

'No dear, I meant the dead man, not the blood-stains.'

'It's not my fault he stabbed himself to death on my knitting. I didn't ask him to!'

Their squabbling was interrupted by the eerie, but unmistakeable, sound of a police radio. They leaned in closer to listen to the message coming from the dead man's jacket pocket.

'Station control to DC Evans, are you reading me? We need to have an urgent update on your whereabouts. Over.'

Outside in the road, a black BMW drew up to the kerb and two young men got out. One of them was carrying a baseball bat. They glanced at the silver car but carried on walking towards Dennis and Sheila's front door

# PANIC ROOM

James's writing challenge for 6th August 2018. Write a story with a twist, not just any twist but a revelation which alters the perception of the story – with the caveat that the twist must be obvious in insight. No more than 1,200 words.

**Commentary:** In 2018 the Ibiza-born indie singer/songwriter Au/Ra released a single called "Panic Room". When I heard it on the radio I was instantly inspired.

---

**FOR SALE** – Unmissable opportunity for the right buyer. A three-bedroom detached home with the unusual addition of a panic room located off the master bedroom suite. Call now in confidence 01376 432189. Matthews-Lynch Agency.

---

Alistair turned to his wife and nudged her arm.

'I wish you wouldn't do that, Alistair. You made me jump.'

'Sorry Fiona, but look at this. It could be the answer. What do you think?'

'Is that a serious advert? What paper are you reading?'

'It's the local rag. I'm going to call the agents. No harm in looking, is there?'

'I don't know. I can't think about it anymore.'

'I think it's worth considering. If it solves the problem, then maybe we can relax a little bit.'

As he stood up from the sofa and walked towards the hall doorway, his wife turned her head to look at him, her eyes questioning, her forehead rippled with frown lines.

'I do trust you,' she said 'If you think it might help, I'll go along with it.'

'I'll be careful, don't worry.'

*****

The estate agency was located off the High Street. Brian Lynch welcomed the couple into the office at 3pm precisely on the Saturday afternoon. He hadn't been expecting many responses to his advertisement, but the prompt reply from this couple had left him optimistic of success.

'Mr and Mrs Duff. Do come in.'

'Do you mind if the door is locked? It would make my wife feel much safer.'

'Of course, and there are no other clients expected today as you expressly requested.'

'We are grateful,' Fiona Duff said. 'I am grateful. I hope you understand why we have to take all these complicated precautions.'

'Quite. A most unusual circumstance but a very unfortunate one for you both.'

'It's not as unusual as you might think. Stalking isn't confined to celebrities, you know.'

'I'm sorry, I don't mean to pry.'

'No, it's best that you know what we are up against, then you'll understand why we will be asking for total confidentiality and tight security. There's no point in us viewing this house if the location isn't kept secret by all involved.'

Alistair took up the story, checking with his wife from time to time to make sure he had all the details straight. He took out a photograph from his jacket pocket and placed it on the table.

'This is the latest likeness we have. It was taken a few months after he came out of prison in January. Fiona's sister saw it in a newspaper report. Despite the beard and the hat, you can make out his features clearly enough. But he could be clean shaven by now. He likes to keep us on our toes.'

'And you're worried he might hurt you again, Mrs Duff. I quite understand your dilemma.'

'I'm worried my ex-husband will try and *kill* me, Mr Lynch. That's what he went to prison for. Unfortunately for me, he pleaded guilty to the lesser charge of attempted manslaughter. The police and that stupid judge who believed his story should be ashamed of how they let me down.'

'It's all right, darling,' Alistair said, 'there's no need to go over all that now. We simply need to make sure that absolute secrecy is maintained throughout the purchase. If we go ahead.'

Brian Lynch sought to reassure the couple. 'I do understand and, subsequent to your phone call, I have removed the property from our listings and nothing will connect you with it, not from our agency, at least.'

Alistair patted his wife's arm. 'And we'll use our own trusted solicitor to do the paperwork, the one who fought for this madman to be put away for the rest of his life. We trust him completely.'

Fiona leaned across the table and looked Brian Lynch directly in the eye. 'All we need to know is … can we trust you to keep our secret?'

'Yes, Mr and Mrs Duff, Alistair and Fiona, your secret is one hundred percent safe with me.'

*****

The sale proceeded without a hitch. There was no upward chain. Alistair told their key worker at Victim Relocation that they'd decided to take charge of their own security and vacate the safe house. He didn't add that the locations of safe houses were traded on the dark web for a few pounds and the local police force leaked like a sieve.

After six weeks of worry, their hopes raised and dashed many times and their nerves frayed to shreds, Alistair received the call from their solicitor. The money had been successfully transferred to the vendor via a holding account in the name of one of the partners. It was time to collect the keys and move in. One final administrative detail remained, to notify the Land Registry. The name of the legal owner would be hidden via a trust, set up to protect Fiona Duff from any intrusive enquiries into her whereabouts.

*****

That same afternoon, Fiona walked through the empty house, reviewing the room sizes and thinking about where she wanted to put the furniture. Her final destination was the master suite. The large and airy bedroom overlooking the back garden was decorated in cool creams and greys. The en-suite was small but well-equipped with a walk-in shower, basin and loo, fully tiled in neutral tones. Stepping back into the bedroom, she turned to the fitted wardrobe. Opening the left-hand unit, she gazed at the hidden door to the spacious and secure panic room. The door was comfortingly solid, the thick metal tight in its frame. It was impenetrable. She would feel safe.

*****

Two weeks later, Fiona again walked through the new house, pleased with the layout, the furnishings, the feeling of homeliness and the sense that she was now exactly where she wanted to be in her life. Her plans, so carefully laid, had finally come to fruition.

She was in the bedroom, looking again at the door to her panic room, when she heard the doorbell ring. She wasn't expecting anyone. Her meticulous preparations precluded the possibility of unwanted visitors.

With Alistair safely stowed in the freezer, cut up into manageable-sized joints – ready for the dogs she would soon be re-homing – she was puzzled as to who would be disturbing her peace. The solicitor was also taken care of, mown down outside his office by a hit-and-run driver of unknown identity, witnesses having yet to come forward. Her idiot ex-husband, the stalker, had been stupid enough to fall headlong into the baited trap she had set for him and was now blue in the face and as dead as a doornail in her (now hermetically-sealed) panic room. Having disconnected the ventilation, it now served as a useful tomb.

With all these visitor possibilities discounted, she wondered again who could possibly be ringing her bell?

Fiona scampered down the stairs, if only to stop the incessant ringing. She opened the door wide and pasted on her most welcoming smile. In front of her was a beautiful bouquet of the most glorious flowers – pink roses, fragrant carnations, delicate alstroemeria and clouds of gypsophilia completing the arrangement. Hovering above the flowers was a face she recognised but had dismissed. Brian Lynch. He smiled. She smiled back. He lowered the flowers and flashed his badge.

'Fiona Duff AKA Andrea Cummings AKA Deirdre Boscombe, I am arresting you on suspicion of the kidnap and murder of Peter Cummings. You do not have to say anything but it may harm your defence if you do not mention, when questioned, something which you later rely on in court. Anything you do say may be given in evidence. I have a search warrant for these premises.' In the background a number of officers stood waiting and watching, witnesses to the drama.

Fiona Duff AKA Andrea Cummings AKA Deirdre Boscombe stood aside and motioned the officers to enter the premises. 'Perhaps you'd all like to begin by checking my panic room,' she said, a smile playing gently around her lips. 'There's plenty of space for everyone to go inside and have a good look around.'

# GOOLDEN VS. HM GOVERNMENT

Chair's writing challenge for 24th September 2018. Write a story of no more than 1,200 words in epistolary (letters and/or emails) or diary form (but not both, nor a mixture of the two forms). Choose your own title.

The story should have at least four letters/emails or four diary entries and must include at least four of the following sentences:

- Yes, I know all about you.
- It may be life but not as we know it.
- [The title of a best-selling book]. Best-selling means sold at least 1m copies.
- Going home is such a lonely ride.
- If I've told you once, I've told you a thousand times.
- And then the [insert creature (dog, bird of paradise, buffalo, archaeopteryx... )] left the room.

- Yesterday, I was happy.
- Why should I believe you?
- If you're ever in a jam, here I am.
- If I can get out of that, I can get out of anything.

**Commentary:** Mike always sets such intriguing challenges and it's wise to think carefully about the piece before you begin. Attention to detail is everything.

Newspapers provide ample inspiration for my stories. The outlandish proclamations of journalists never fail to spark my imagination. No doubt some inflammatory account of the prison service coupled with a damning rebuke from a human rights lawyer provided the springboard for my response to this challenge.

*****

Balfour Chambers
43 Lincoln's Inn
London
14th July 2021

Dear Mr Goolden

I refer to my letter of 3rd June with regard to your upcoming case. We now have a date for the full hearing which will take place at the High Court on 14th October. I have duly written to the authorities, including the Governor of Ashley Fields, to formally request that you are given leave to attend your hearing in person.

I hope this good news will allow you to see that there is an end within sight to the clear injustice you are suffering in Ashley Fields.

My assistant, Alison Mason will be in to visit next week to go over the final details of your testimony. If you have any further questions, Alison will be able to help you.

Yours sincerely

Michael Whittaker QC

\*\*\*\*\*

Amadeo Laboratories
Cambourne Business Park
Cambridge
26th July 2021

Lab Report – Case 459, High Court

Dear Ms Mason

Please find enclosed our final report into the Securibot Model 3C. The key findings you should note are on page 28. If you compare the parameters of response we have listed in the columns, it should be clear that the 3C is, in our view, insufficiently developed to cope with the challenges of the environment in which it is being deployed.

Taking these results together with the published data on this model, our report should assist with the above case. I am reminded of the wise words which have passed into colloquial use – 'It may be life, but not as we know it.' I think that phrase sums up the test results.

If we are required to give evidence in person, please refer to the fee schedule included with this letter.

We wish you and your client all success. You will receive our invoice in due course.

Kieran Voles, Technical Director

*****

Balfour Chambers
43 Lincoln's Inn
London
14th July 2021

Dear Mr Goolden

Michael Whittaker has asked me to send you a summary of the case notes and the arguments we will use to try and establish that your fundamental human rights are being harmed by the regime at Ashley Fields. I hope you will see that we have amassed some strong evidence which I attach. We are confident that the arguments will work in your favour.

You may have noticed that there is considerable public interest in your plight. The fund to cover your costs now stands at an impressive 82.6K in Bit coin which will more than cover the fees and court costs. I will, in due course, send you an updated account which covers all our expenses to date.

I was moved by our meeting last week and your assertion that you consider this struggle is your own personal battle against the malign and insidious creep of Artificial Intelligence into every aspect of our daily lives. However, your heartfelt plea that you will 'Die Trying' is perhaps overly pessimistic because your release date, in any event, will be January 2023.

In view of the nature of the case and the immediate proximity to yourself of the robotic prison officer, I'm sure I have no need to remind you of the importance of caution in everything you do and say. Please keep all documents away from prying eyes.

Everyone at Balfour Chambers is rooting for you, so let's look forward to a successful outcome. I will be in touch again soon.

Yours sincerely

Alison Mason

\*\*\*\*\*

Balfour Chambers
43 Lincoln's Inn
London
9th September 2021

Dear Mr Goolden

I'm writing to appraise you about a significant development in your case. You may not be aware of this as I know you refuse to watch any sort of electronic device or television as part of your campaign against technology, therefore this news may not have reached you. I enclose a paper copy of the report which has been playing out in the electronic media all week.

The Justice Secretary, the Rt. Hon. Ian Williams, has been forced to resign following the revelations that he has financial links to the manufacturers of the Securibot Model 3C and stands to make a considerable fortune out of its wide deployment in the prison service. This has, to coin a phrase, set the cat among the pigeons. A full review is now to take place into the scheme to use robotic prison guards to replace human officers. There have been further reports of similar concerns that you raised into the way the Securibot Model 3C lacks so much basic humanity that prisoners' fundamental rights are being undermined. There is more detail in the article I have enclosed so I will leave you to read it in your own time. With this in mind, I have asked for the postponement of the case because a judge will not make a ruling while the investigation is ongoing. However, I am optimistic that matters will resolve themselves soon.

You have been instrumental in exposing a serious political scandal and have also raised vital questions about the viability of AI robots having sole control of the prison system.

Miss Mason sends her regards. She said, while raising a glass of champagne in your honour, 'The Justice Secretary was the elephant in the room and the elephant has left the room. For good!'

I will keep you informed.

Yours sincerely

Michael Whittaker QC

*****

HMP Ashley Fields
Norfolk
13th September 2021

Dear Mum

It now looks like I'm going to be banged up with this robot until my normal release date. The lawyers wrote to me and said there has been a scandal and the case has been postponed. The robot sniggered when I read the letter and said it served me right for questioning AI progress. That's what they always say when people in here get annoyed. It told me, 'Don't question the AI project, it's the future whether you like it or not.'

You asked what happened to that money people donated, well it seems the lawyers spent it all on their fees and the costs of doing the investigations. Anyway, it wasn't money we could spend. It was raised to fight for my release.

Come and visit me as soon as you can, Mum. I need some human company. Bring me some more books. Until then I just have my robot to talk to. I have called him Gwendolyn to annoy him. Maybe I'll spend the rest of my sentence getting up the metallic nose of my constant companion and jailor, Gwendolyn. It will give me something to bother waking up for. Yesterday I was happy, now I'm just resigned to my fate.

Your loving son, Alan

# THE BIDDENHAM GHOSTS

A short story written for the NWI 2018 anthology, *And Ghosts Are Real, Too*.

**Commentary:** The brief for the *And Ghosts Are Real, Too* anthology was to write a story based around Wellingborough, the location of the group, or to locate your tale in your own home town, because some members come from other areas. The theme, either a number of short pieces or a longer story, should be on the subject of ghosts, horror or crime. I chose to write one piece for my full word count of about 4,000 words.

The village where I live is very haunted. As two family members are rather sensitive to super-natural entities, this has made our time here quite challenging on occasions. Ghostly activities in our home tend to happen in clusters. Sometimes at night it's possible to see and sense a darkness moving across the bedroom. Sometimes you might wake in the night thinking that somebody is calling your name. Or you see a person you don't recognise standing in the doorway looking at you. Perhaps such occurrences are imagined or a product of dreams. However, the regularity of these events has made us rather blasé about them. My elder daughter has even joked that when she sees a ghost in her room, she points to the wardrobe and says, 'The portal's that way. Off you go.' Because some research and listening to tales in the village have led us to conclude that there may be a portal close by and our home just happens to be en-route for travelling souls who are recently departed. And if you wake in the night with a dark shape staring at you while you sleep, it's not necessarily a cause for alarm, just an opportunity to provide some helpful directions, if required. The recently departed don't seem to have satnav.

Our own departed pets often make an appearance, either seen out of the corner of your eye or heard somewhere in the house. We hear the familiar sound of a dog's collar and identity tag clinking together as a ghostly canine walks through the rooms of their former home. A long departed cat sometimes waits to be let out of the back door or to be let into a bedroom at night to sleep on the bed (even though it wasn't allowed when the cat was alive). We have an image taken by an external security camera, angled into the lounge through the patio windows that feature in this story. Sitting on the carpet, staring up at the television, is our old ginger cat Nigel who departed many years ago.

Experience has taught me that paranormal entities are rarely seen "head on". They are more likely to be seen in peripheral vision which seems more sensitive to the subtle visual changes that occur in the presence of non-physical entities. Other senses then come into play, the auditory and kinaesthetic senses. And also that sense of knowing – almost a primitive understanding – that something is wrong and there might be danger. That's when you feel the hairs on the back of your neck stand up.

In this story I have used personal experiences and mixed them with local folklore to tell a tale of a young girl being haunted. I hope the narrative gives you a good fright. I also wanted to indulge in some atmospheric scene setting which is not my usual style, but is appropriate to this story.

*****

**In the depths of the countryside**, away from the ochre glow of urban streetlights, darkness settles on the landscape like a black shroud on a corpse. Pavements shift and become insubstantial, buildings hug the land, seeking the solid earth to guard themselves from night-time uncertainties. Trees creak and sway as the wind gusts through their branches. Skies darken and blanket everything with gloom. A waning crescent moon reveals unlikely shadows as the scudding clouds part and then swiftly close up again.

The night bustles with nocturnal creatures. A fox, sprightly after a blood-soaked feast, trots replete across the field to its lair. A Muntjac deer barks for its mate, then creeps deeper into the woodland to wait. A field mouse, nimble and silent, scampers up a bird table, huddling down to avoid the piercing talons of the owl as it swoops towards the oak trees. Two cats, locked in a stand-off, fur raised, bodies arched, back away and run towards their homes and the prospect of a warm bed by the fire.

The pub, The Three Casks, turns out its reluctant regulars and the landlord drapes towels over the pumps. The door is locked and the lights are extinguished. His wife calls him up to their cosy apartment. He then sets the intruder alarm before ascending the stairs. Outside in the pub car park, two gentlemen douse their final cigarettes, plunging them into the sand bucket by the door, before muttering farewells and walking unsteadily into the night.

Tonight is an ordinary night. Behind the floral curtains of cottages and barns, residents bank up the Aga, stir mugs of Horlicks or settle on a well-deserved tot of rum to send them off to the land of nod. Or up the stairs to Bedfordshire as they often say, whenever the fancy takes them.

The village road curves around wide verges then splits into two, bisecting a triangle of green space that houses the village sign. One road disappears towards the church, the other heads towards the main road. Dusk Cottage, which overlooks the small green, is nestled under a thickly thatched roof and secured by an arched oak door, strong with black rivets. An estate agent's board announces it is "For Sale". Empty rooms lie behind the thin curtains. Cold grates wait for a new owner to light a fire.

To the right of this cottage, a hand-painted signpost points to the path that leads to the village pond. This path is the Coffin Path, known to be the most direct route from the old village morgue, located in the garden of The Three Casks, towards the church and the chance of a proper Christian burial. When sturdy men would be obliged to carry the deceased the half-mile towards the church of St. James, the shortest path was always preferred.

Coffin Path is dark and empty. Recent rain has made the nettles surge. Muddy paw and foot prints lead towards the silent pond. The path then creeps further into the night and away towards its final resting place in the church yard. As if on cue, the church bell sounds eleven o'clock.

Dusk Cottage stands foursquare on its plot, the foundations of brine-soaked ship's timbers forming the frame and bonding it with the bare earth it stands on. Yet, if you looked closely enough and knew what to look for, you'd notice a loose copper strip dangling by the front door. This copper strip, glinting in the moonlight, has become disconnected from the thick copper spike that's been plunged into the dark soil nearby. If you understood the meaning of this breakage, you'd knot your brows and wonder nervously about the consequences. But that would require you to have a deeper understanding of the natural order of things, both in this world and the next. You'd have to be aware of the subtle energies of earth, water, fire and air, of the energy lines that criss-cross the land and transmit a signal to those who can sense it. This disconnection would trouble you. You'd know that the balance was upset. The deep energies that lie inside the earth cannot flow when transmission channels are disrupted. Instead of flowing away towards other villages and intersections, flowing unhindered towards centres of great significance, those ancient energies now pool and spread out, brooding and spiteful, around the mouth of Coffin Path.

*****

'Who is that walking by the War Memorial? Do you know them?' The woman said as she tugged on her dog's lead.

'Where? Actually, is there anybody there? I can't see anybody,' her companion replied.

'You're right. It's the odd light at this time of day. I've seen a strange woman hanging around, though. Definitely not someone that I recognise from the village.'

'I think I know who you mean. She said hello to me the other day at the post box. Her family have just moved into The Old Vicarage.'

'How interesting.'

'And she's not strange, she's quite normal and friendly. The family have moved here from abroad somewhere, I'm not quite sure where. They have two children and her name is Kate.'

'Mystery solved, then.'

'I wouldn't want to live in that house.'

'The Old Vicarage? No, me neither. It depends on whether or not you can see dead people, I suppose.'

'I'm told it's much worse if you can feel them. More creepy.'

'Well, let's face it, in this village, you get plenty of opportunity for both.'

'Let's turn around at the bus shelter, I don't feel like going to the pond tonight.'

'Fine, let's get these dogs home before it gets dark.'

*****

Sophie puts her sandwich down on the side table and turns on the television. She has some programmes recorded that her dad thinks are rubbish. If she doesn't watch them when she has the chance, he'll delete them. She settles down to watch Paranormal Lockdown. The investigators are due to be locked into a long-disused mental hospital for 72 hours in this episode.

The dogs barge through the lounge door and settle alongside her on the sofa. They will do anything for food and believe the last bits of a sandwich crust are theirs by right.

'There, eat up and that's your lot. Now you can get down. Go on, get down both of you.'

Charlie, the flat-coated retriever, ignores her and sneaks away to snuggle under a cushion but Ollie, a border collie, obediently gets down and takes up his normal position by the front window.

Sophie thinks about getting up to close the curtains and block out the night but can't be bothered. The large front windows look out over a small enclosed garden with honey stone paving and an ivy covered stone wall. Although it's pitch dark outside and the blackness makes the room less cosy, she needs early warning of her parents return so she can get out her schoolbooks and pretend she's been revising. From where she sits, any car headlights coming towards the house will be visible.

She clicks play on her recording. Charlie starts to snore loudly. She turns the volume up. Ollie twitches in his sleep. On the television, the lockdown is in progress and the team are bedding down in the operating theatre. That's where they expect to detect the most paranormal activity. They have already set up night vision cameras, electronic voice recorders and electromagnetic detection devices. They also have a spirit box, but not just any old spirit box. They are testing a new device that projects magnetic resonance in lines forming a grid the size of the human body. The theory is that a dead person could use the energy to manifest inside the box.

Sophie is spellbound as the gridwork lights up the operating theatre with spectral blues and greens, casting strangely shaped shadows on the walls and ceiling. To accompany the light show, the spirit box makes an unearthly noise – a series of bangs, crackles and thumps.

'Holy shit,' one of the presenters shouts, 'it's already picking up a demonic presence.'

'Step away from it, the energy is building.'

'What the hell is that? Did you push me?'

'Something really evil is in the room with us. I'm feeling sick and dizzy.'

'Were in trouble here guys. Stop the spirit box! Turn it off!'

Sophie sits entranced watching the action. Then out of nowhere the TV screen goes blank and the house is plunged into darkness. All Sophie can see are the faint outlines of the furniture and the eerie glow of moonlight from the window. She is seriously annoyed and she sits for a while, hoping the power will soon come back on again. She wonders when her parents will come back, then tries to remember where the fuse box is located and how she might check to find out if a circuit has shorted out.

'You are so not helping,' she says to the dogs.

Neither dog seems bothered by the darkness. Sophie crawls off the sofa and crouches down at the fireplace. Her hand finds one of the jars containing a scented candle. She fumbles in the log basket and locates the box of matches. Striking the match and lighting the candle, she sits back on her haunches, feeling pleased she's done something useful. She then lights another two candles.

'That's cosy. Now what do we do, dogs? Come on. Let's find my phone.'

Upstairs, the floorboards creak.

'No way,' she mutters to herself.

Sophie looks down at the floor and notices that Ollie has raised his head off the carpet. Charlie is still buried under a cushion. The disembodied creaking continues. Her voice dies in her throat as she strains her ears to listen. These noises are not recognisable as ordinary, *heating coming on* creaks. She detects the sound of an equally re-cognisable creaking – a *person walking slowly on the upstairs landing*. The top step groans. It always does. She realises she knows exactly how every footstep sounds in this old house. This noise, she realises, is of somebody or something coming down the stairs.

Ollie sits up, his head cocked to one side in the candlelight. She sees his lips curl back, revealing his large, white teeth. A low rumble sounds in his chest. Sophie holds her breath.

Then the lights flash back on and the telephone bleeps and the television comes back on. Ollie stares at the lounge door, his hackles stiff and his body hunched, ready to pounce.

That's when she screams.

\*\*\*\*\*

'Did you get a power cut last night?'

'No, did you?'

'Well, we did it seems. Sophie was totally freaked out by the time I came home, saying something about noises on the stairs.'

'Sounds scary.'

'Not what you need when the electricity goes off and you're alone in the house.'

'Is she all right?'

'Yes, back to normal but we had to spend some time reassuring her. We walked up and down the stairs and across the landing a few times. Nothing like the noises she heard, apparently. I think it was just a coincidence that the heating pipes were cooling down or heating up when the power went off.'

'Our house creaks all the time and it's only five years old.'

'That's new-build housing for you. How far do you want to walk today?'

'Let's go by the side road onto the golf course. Give the dogs a nice run.'

*****

Sophie lies on one side of her double bed looking at the shadows on the ceiling, thinking about how frightened she was when the power went off. She can hear the familiar murmur of her parents talking downstairs as they make a bedtime drink and put the dogs to bed. Then she thinks about Ollie and how terrified he was. She's never seen him like that. Her heart speeds up and she has to concentrate on her breathing to get herself calmed down. She pulls the duvet closer and tucks her nose under the covers. She hears the front door being locked and the downstairs lights being switched off. The glow from her bedroom doorway dims.

'Goodnight, darling.'

'Night Mum, Dad.'

'See you in the morning.'

Sleep blurs the senses and makes reality seem insubstantial. Sophie wakes in the night, her feet tangled up inside the duvet. The house is quiet. She reaches down and tugs the cover away. Then she notices that something's not quite right on the other side of the bed. There's a weight, pressing down, a dead weight. As if somebody is sitting on that side. Or it could be a dog. But Ollie and Charlie are in the kitchen, she knows that for certain.

'Mum,' she whispers.

Or maybe she just thought the word in her head. She can't decide because her heart is thumping so loud the noise is deafening.

She daren't move.

She daren't breathe.

She daren't think.

Then it happens. The weight moves and lifts. There's a muffled sound of footsteps on the carpet, padding softly in the direction of her wardrobe. Then nothing, the room is silent.

This time she finds she can't scream.

*****

'I met that woman Kate today, the one I told you about. Really nice lady. She's putting both her girls into the village school after half-term.'

'Good, that'll boost the numbers.'

'Found out some interesting things about the house. Things even I didn't know.'

'Do tell me.'

'It seems they did some in depth research before they decided to buy it. When it was the actual rectory, apparently they buried the stillborn babies in the garden. It was normal practice when infant mortality was high.'

'I hope there aren't any dead babies in our garden.'

'But your house is a barn so there will only be dead sheep or pigs or whatever.'

'Thank you for pointing that out.'

'That's just how it is. She told me that one of the rectors lost about eleven or twelve babies. Really sad. The stillborns weren't allowed to be buried in the churchyard as they hadn't been baptised.'

'That is very sad, it seems quite unchristian by today's standards.'

'Little lost souls, so many little lost souls.'

*****

Darkness plays on your mind when you are afraid. There are no streetlights in this part of the village. People boast about how they prefer the darkness. No light pollution cluttering up the sky and interfering with the stars. How Sophie longs for some comforting streetlights.

She's spending another evening at home. It's a chance to watch a recorded programme while her mother is at a committee meeting and her father is having a drink at the pub. Both of them are only five minutes away. But the darkness doesn't care about that as it creeps closer.

The creaking on the stairs – she is now used to it. It can't be explained but she's used to it. The night terrors are not so easy to cope with. She doesn't broach the subject with her parents. She can't make the words come out of her mouth. To do that will make it real. Once the words have been said, they cannot be taken back. Anyway, what can anyone do?

She invites the dogs onto the sofa and cuddles them close, bribing them with a digestive biscuit. Then she puts on the extra light by the sideboard and wills herself to calm down. The television is turned up loud, loud enough to drown out any sounds that she doesn't want to hear. The dogs are her barometer. She strokes them and checks that they are relaxed. Earlier that evening, she shut the curtains but it didn't make her feel any safer. The room closed in, claustrophobic, so she opened them again.

Ollie lays across her lap, dribbling onto her sleeve. The television show plays out on the screen, the flashing lights reflected faintly in the window. Something catches her eye outside the house. She notices somebody in her peripheral vision walking along the road. She dismisses it as one of the neighbour's children or a visiting friend. A pale blond blur of hair moves above the stone garden wall, almost disembodied. The dogs snore and twitch, both unimpressed.

She concentrates on the TV programme. She has to concentrate to keep the fear at bay. The flash of lights, the canned laughter and the inane presenting all help to take her mind off what might be happening upstairs on the landing. Then she hears the sound of a familiar car. A door slams and she hears the bleep of a remote control. Her mother's head appears over the stone wall and she waves to Sophie. Her mother's head, visible and lit up by the security light on the drive. Clear and crisp and real.

Sophie focuses on the front window and notices again how the television screen is reflected in the window glass. And then a shutter snaps open inside her head. A deep, knowing part of her understands that the pale head she had seen earlier had not been outside the room, walking in the road in front of the garden wall. Her skin begins to crawl. She forces herself to look back into the room, past the book cases, towards the far wall with the huge mirror. And she realises that what she had seen earlier was a disembodied head walking from one side of the living room to the other, reflected in the glass of the window.

*****

Sophie lies in the darkness, dreading the arrival of the weight on her bed, the silent, brooding weight. She is powerless to stop it happening. It is now her secret. She cannot explain it or speak about it.

Inside the cocoon of her bed, she listens for the other sounds, the ones she knows will follow. The creak of the floorboard outside her bedroom door. The swish, as if the hem of a silky dress is dragging along the carpet. The sudden tap of an invisible knuckle on her wardrobe door. Then the padding footfalls inside her room. She knows that she is being watched. There is no shock, not like in the films or the TV programmes she used to love so much. Just the horrifying inevitability that soon, one night very soon, whatever is in the room will come for her.

*****

By the Coffin Path, the darkness intensifies. A late dog walker, carrying a useful torch, thinks better of turning down towards the pond and sticks with the footpath that takes him towards the main road.

Talk in the public bar of The Three Casks turns to the strangers seen around the village of late. There is disagreement over who they might be.

'I've no idea what you're talking about, mate. Haven't seen anyone I didn't know.'

'Come on, John. Every evening I see them, same clothes, really rough looking. Hanging around by the War Memorial or on the way to the pond.'

'It'll be ramblers, some of them look like they dressed in the dark. Or that Nordic walking group that Glenys belongs to.'

'They look really odd, like from another time.'

'I still don't know what you're on about.'

*****

Sophie dreads going into her bedroom. She does her homework at the kitchen table. She clings to her mother's arm when it's her bedtime. Inside her head, her voice screams, *Please help me. I don't know what to do. I'm so scared.* But she mutely does as she has always done and kisses her parents, then walks up the stairs to her bedroom. Her feet are made of lead.

She follows her routine. Zipped tight inside her onesie, she pulls the duvet over her face and inhales the scent of fear. She mutters a few words of prayer to a God she doesn't understand. Then she waits, hoping that she will fall asleep before the landing lights go out.

She awakens to the sound of the church clock striking three in the morning. She keeps her body still, breathing silently, fighting the urge to peek out from under her covers. There is a soft light creeping into her room, a warm comforting kind of light. Then she notices her bed feels normal again. She's alone. She moves her hand over the pillow and lifts her head a fraction. The bedroom door is open.

'Sophie. Sophie.'

Someone is calling her. She squeezes her eyes shut tight but the light seems to penetrate inside her mind.

'Come with me, Sophie.'

And all at once her body is weightless, floating out of her bed, towards the ragged figure of a young woman who beckons her. A woman who smiles with crooked, blackened teeth. Whose hooked finger compels her to come closer until she is flying out of the window, out into the sky. Her house is below her, becoming smaller and smaller. They are speeding up, away towards the road. The village oak trees are beneath her, and within a few moments she sees they are disappearing into the distance. And she feels ... nothing.

There are other ragged figures in the air, other people who are dressed in all sorts of strange and dishevelled clothing. They are floating around and seem to be drifting aimlessly. Their unseeing eyes flit backwards and forwards, as if these creatures are searching for something. The night-time sky is alive with spectres, some huddled in groups, others flying randomly about as if lost.

Then Sophie notices a pale glow in the distance. She feels a tug of happiness. The light grows large and brightens and she finds herself flying fast towards it. It's all around her. And she hears the chatter of excited voices in her head.

'We've found it at last, we can all go now. We can go home. Sophie has shown us the way. She must come with us.'

***** 

Sophie turns over in bed. The bright light has gone and there's a calm voice talking to her. It's a familiar voice although it doesn't seem to be her mother or her father or anyone she knows.

'Stay still and quiet,' the voice says. 'Pull the duvet back over your head and wait.'

And beside her, unmistakeably, the weight is on the side of her bed again.

The church clock strikes four. An owl hoots outside her bedroom window. The weight settles and she notices it's like an anchor, securing her down to the earth.

She wriggles further towards it and finds comfort in its heaviness. Her terrible dream is still fresh in her mind but, for now, all is well.

*****

'Have you had any trouble recently with your ghosts? I meant to ask you the other day,' says the woman with the Labrador.

'Now you mention it, I think we have,' replies her companion, tugging her Jack Russell away from the scent of fox. 'The house has been feeling distinctly unsettled of late. Like they are agitated and we've had a few mishaps like broken dishes and the toaster went kaput.'

'I was talking to the vicar about it. His ghosts have been moaning on at him all day and night. Complaining that the departed are not moving on as they should. He mentioned that we might have to get those psychic people back, the ones who re-routed the ley line.'

'What on earth are you talking about?'

'Oh, I thought it was common knowledge. The ley line that runs through the village but gets stuck at Dusk Cottage and again at the church. The vicar says we need to get the energy flowing again so all these dead people who want to pass over can find their way to the nearest portal. It's like a meeting point for departed souls. It's over by the sharp bend on the main road. Where they used to hang up the highwaymen'

'You seem to know a lot about it.'

'Only what the vicar told me but I suppose most of the people who have lived here a long time know about it.'

'And you say it's where they used to hang up the highwaymen?'

'Yes, I think it used to be called Gallows Corner.'

'So why aren't all the dead people going to this portal thingy?'

'Oh, didn't I explain? The village ley line acts like a conduit helping departed souls to move swiftly towards their final destination. If it's blocked or weak, the souls lose their way. My ghosts have been up in arms about it, moaning and whinging. Saying they can't get any peace and quiet with all these disoriented dead people cluttering the place up.'

'I suppose it's rather like having your unwanted relatives to stay and you can't get rid of them.'

'Exactly. So have yours been playing up lately? Everyone I speak to says the same thing. Lots of agitated ghosts.'

'And what can be done about it, again?'

'Well, we get the psychic people back and they trace the energy all along the ley line for any obstructions or breakages. They use special copper wire to re-route around any blockages. Perhaps they'll find that somebody has built a new extension or dug up their drains or something. Then they get the energy whooshing along and everyone is happy again. The living and the dead and the ghosts who just prefer to hang around in our houses for the fun of it.'

'I hope it works. My ghosts are getting distinctly restless.'

'It'll work fine; these psychic types know what they're doing. Parish Council will pay, of course.'

'Goodness, is that what they use the village precept for?

'And the roads, Deidre, and the cricket pitch and mowing the verges and don't forget about the village show.'

\*\*\*\*\*

Sophie lies in a beam of sunshine with her hand gently smoothing and stroking the covers on the right hand side of her bed. As she strokes, she can feel the unseen presence shift and move around. Then they touch. It feels like nothing more than the ripple of a breeze making her hand tingle. And she is comforted.

Sophie now has everything all worked out in her mind. The extraordinary flying dream. The peculiar people she met. The huge welcoming light in the sky and the strange voices that she heard, telling her things. Unbelievable things. During one fateful night she joined the souls of the departed on their journey onwards to whatever lies in that light. But her heart told her that it wasn't her time. It wasn't her journey.

Now she doesn't need to worry about the footsteps in her room or the swish of a dress on her carpet. This is her special secret. She has her own spirit protector who kept her safe that night.

She doesn't have to tell anyone about the dream or what she knows. Because she's realised that most people, even her mum and dad, already seem to know. It's the talk of the village.

# AUTUMN LEAVES

Pat's writing assignment for 5th November 2018. Choose one picture from the selection at the end of these notes and write a story of up to 1200 words inspired by it. They are:

- a picture of a lighthouse, with a man leaning up against it,
- a picture of a little girl walking into the woods — see below.

Photo by Gary Ellis on Unsplash

**Commentary:** Imagine towns and cities where nature has been obliterated. Where only concrete and technology exist. Where people never go outside and the only cars on the road are driven by invisible software. Imagine a child, sneaking out of her house and discovering a tree for the first time.

*****

**Outside the house,** where the breeze ruffled her hair, where the light made her screw up her eyes, the child slowed and took a long breath. Hands on hips, she stood in the street, unsure about where to go next. A backward glance told her she'd come further than ever before.

Under her feet, the grey pavement stretched away. She concentrated on walking in the middle of each slab to avoid the cracks. On her left, a pale smooth wall of stone hemmed her in. On her right, the road marched onwards, dark and smooth and empty. The quiet sky closed its greyness over her head and brooded.

The aloneness made her feel anxious. But she took a deep breath and kept up the walking rhythm along the pavement. A car whirred along beside her. The sound of the tyres on the road crept closer, then it passed by. No driver. On its way to collect someone or deliver something.

Down by her feet was a leaf, red and gold and yellow, curling at the edges. She bent and picked it up. She knew it was a leaf because she'd once read a story about things called trees. Some trees were green all the time and some changed their colours. They grew out of the ground. They were alive but not in the same way that people were. Never having touched a leaf before, she tenderly smoothed over the shiny surface with her small fingers, tracing the sharp edges around to the dry stalk. It was too big to put in her pocket so she held it between two fingers.

The smooth pale stone wall ended and cold wind rippled over her face, bringing a new scent that was light and fresh and alive. Around the corner, surrounded by black railings, was a real tree. She took a few steps back to look at it properly. It was moving in time with the wind. The leaves rustled and swayed, one or two dropping gently to the ground. She reached out and caught them.

The wind strengthened and more leaves fluttered to the ground. She swished her feet through them and felt the gladness overtake her. Leaves were entangled in her hair. They rested on the shoulders of her coat and tucked themselves into the top of her boots. The air turned yellow and orange and red.

The grey pavement, such a familiar part of her existence so far, seemed to melt away. In its place was soft, brown squishy earth. She ran, kicking up tufts of grass. She jumped, landing in puddles of water. Her coat flew open and the bright, fresh air filled her up.

On either side of the path were great banks of many different leaves. It was heavenly to jump headfirst and feel the springy mattress of the fallen leaves break her fall. She rubbed handfuls of them together and watched the fragments trickle through her fingers. The crackling sound was magical. Her eyes were filled with colour. Her mind was alive with wonder. She sat in her pile of leaves and gazed about, unable to make herself feel afraid, despite the fading light.

Then through the trees she saw movement and light. There were people in the distance, walking and skipping and jumping. A homely-looking woman, dressed in greens and browns, led a band of children out onto the path. Two of the younger ones scampered towards her.

'She's here, Mother. She's here already. Didn't you tell us so?'

The woman approached. 'Now then children, don't crowd too close,' she said as she held up her lantern which illuminated her rosy cheeks and twinkly eyes. 'Hello young miss, we're very glad you've finally arrived. Did your journey go well?'

'My journey? Oh, I only went out of my house for a little while ... but then I saw the leaf ... and ...'

'And the leaves were so beautiful, weren't they?'

'So many beautiful colours! I've never seen so many colours before.'

'And the leaves brought you here to us. We've been expecting you.'

The kindly woman held out her hands and the child reached out, climbing up from her leafy bed. The other children clustered around, smiling and patting her, touching her face and whispering to each other.

The woman bent down and put her warm hands on the child's shoulders, speaking soft words into her ears, saying. 'You've now come home to us. Whatever led you away from your other life has brought you here. I am the Mother and these little scamps are just some of the children. We hope you'll come to love us as we already love you. Now, we'll get back to the farm and perhaps you'd like to help with feeding the chickens and putting them into the barn for the night. By then we'll have our dinner on the table and you can warm yourself by the fire.'

'Mother, Mother. Tell her about her name,' one of the children said.

'Oh, yes. If it pleases you, the children decided you should be called Autumn.'

And because the gladness in her heart had grown so big and because the memory of the grey and the emptiness and the silence of her other life was already dissolving so fast, Autumn nodded her head and smiled so hard it hurt her cheeks.

\*\*\*\*\*

Far away and several hours later, where the grey had swamped all life and nature and freshness, another mother lifted her eyes from her phone. In the climate-controlled concrete box home, she glanced towards the chair where her child had been left to play games on an interactive pad. The chair was vacant. Before she could find out where the child had gone to, the phone pinged and her attention was diverted back towards the screen.

# GABRIEL'S MESSAGE

This piece was written for the meeting of 28th November 2018. It was the anonymous critiquing of members' pieces meeting. We received eight pieces, all stripped of writers' identification marks and unified in terms of font, spacing and so on. After each piece, critiquing followed. This is the only meeting where criticism does not have to be tempered with any positive encouragement. It's no holds barred! And the author of each story can join in the carnage. At the end, everyone has to guess who wrote which piece.

**Commentary:** When I wrote this piece, Christmas preparations were in full swing and there were carols playing on the radio. I suspect that I heard Gabriel's Message as I was seeking inspiration. The opening lines made me think about how events might unfold if an angel visited our modern world. This line caught my attention:

'His wings as drifted snow, his eyes as flame.'

The phrase hints at the terrifying magnificence of this messenger from God.

My mind is also often distracted by thoughts of how messed up the world is. That's the only reason I can give for this dark and, ultimately, destructive story. As you splutter into your mulled wine, try to imagine what Archangel Gabriel might be thinking now if he looked down upon Earth, over 2000 years after he delivered his shocking message to Mary.

*****

**A ruffle of feathers in space**. The faint sound of the movement of wings, stretching out ... and then folding again. Gabriel slowly lifted his head from his chest and opened one eye. A blaze of light shot across the emptiness.

Statuesque and suspended in space, the angel unfurled his wings, uncurled his form and drew himself up to his full, astonishing, height. His wintry gaze took in the vastness of the All-That-Is. His noble head, crowned with a halo of stars, turned to survey the realms of the physical Universe.

'It is time.' The words formed on his proud lips and echoed outwards into space. Waves of sound spread in the direction of Earth and towards his intended audience. A bolt of lightning split the sky and his trumpet appeared in his left hand. Light, blinding light, exploded from around his form. As he spread his wings to fly, the very fabric of time and space trembled.

He journeyed forth, dispensing with galaxies and constellations, slicing through solar systems and bending light as he sped towards his destination. At last, he alighted on a cloud of space dust nestling on the borders of the planetary system containing the world known as Earth. This was not his first visit.

He observed the blue-green colouring of the orb and remembered it was due to the lushness of the beautiful landscape of this world. The endless oceans and the immeasurable grass-filled plains, the barren deserts and desolate icy wastes at both poles. All he surveyed was punctuated at intervals by ragged mountains with snowy caps. He waited, closely observing the human subjects of his current mission.

*****

Gabriel's vigil lasted for many revolutions of the Moon, after which time he held his trumpet to his lips and blew a fanfare that rocked the foundations of the planet's surface, sending clouds of grey dust into the atmosphere. He had only to form his message into thoughts and it was transmitted with total clarity into every mind of every human being who abided there.

And Gabriel beheld the results of his message which, for some of the human population, was fear and confusion and guilt and repentance. But he also observed the vast majority who merely experienced resentment and bitterness and disbelief and arrogance. And it was then that he knew his journey had not been in vain. He had but one final step to complete. And so he asked the question: 'Who will speak for the people of Earth?'

A clamour rose up, consisting of the massed shouts and cries of the inhabitants of the planet. And all Gabriel could hear in that moment was 'Me, me, me.'

Rising sweetly above that base noise was one pure voice, the voice of a child, calling out to be heard above the din. Gabriel held out his arm and spirited the child away, taking her back to the dust cloud where he rested.

The child sat upon his right arm and she also gazed down upon the Earth planet that she called home. Gabriel filled her mind with words, ideas and reasoning. He entreated her, in her purity, to plead the cause of humankind.

'Are you from heaven?' the child asked, her eyes wide with wonder.

Gabriel placed images in her mind of everything that is good and pure and compassionate and worthy, helping her to understand what the word "heaven" might mean.

'Was it your voice that I heard in my head?'

The angel nodded and ruffled his wing feathers.

'Am I in trouble? You sounded so angry.'

Gabriel paused for a moment to adjust his tone for the innocent one. Yet within her mind he noted there was already much wisdom and understanding for the travails of Earth and the wrongs that were routinely perpetrated by her own species.

Then he said, 'It is for the planet that I grieve and all the natural wonders thereon. Mankind was created to have dominion over all things, over the air, water, minerals, plants and all God's creatures. Yet man continues to abuse this power.'

'I know. It makes me so sad. But what can be done about it? I'm just a girl. Nobody would take any notice of me,' the child whispered. If they had not been in space, perhaps a tear would have rolled down her cheek.

Gabriel answered, 'What therefore would you have me do?'

And because the child felt everything so deeply that the angel had shown her and because she could easily imagine the pain and misery inflicted on her home planet by humankind, she looked sweetly into the angel's eyes and said, 'Go ahead. Wipe them out.'

Which is what Gabriel had always intended to do.

'I have one question,' said the girl. 'Are we going to heaven now?'

'Of course, can you not already feel your wing buds growing?'

'Oh, that tickles.'

'Yes it does, but you'll soon get used to it.'

# A GLIMPSE OF WHAT LIES BEYOND

Jason's writing assignment for 7th January 2019. What happens immediately after you die? You have up to 800 words to tell a story, either from the point of view of those you leave behind or the dead person themselves.

**Commentary:** I feel I am on familiar ground when it comes to death and the afterlife. It would have been easy to write more about ghosts but in this case I was inspired by the idea of souls comforting their loved ones after death.

*****

**The envelope appeared on the mantelpiece** one night in May. I'm certain I hadn't noticed it before. The flap was open so I looked inside, drawing out a crisp, cream sheet of paper. On it, written in Sarah's distinctive script, was a name and address in the town. I stood, breathless and unbelieving, waiting for some logic or meaning to present itself. But the envelope was real, the writing real and the blue ink as clear as if Sarah had written it just minutes before.

It took me several days to gather enough courage to drive to the location. It was a quiet road of attractive houses with well-kept gardens. I parked outside number 34. The age Sarah was when she was taken from me. I had no need to knock as the door was already open. I entered, noticing the light scent of fresh flowers and the feeling of being at home, although I had never been there before.

I was drawn towards the back of the house where I could hear a female voice talking quietly. At a table sat a young woman, her lovely face turned towards mine. She smiled and gestured that I should sit opposite her.

'Are you ... is this ...?' I stuttered.

'No need to talk,' she said, her voice light and silky. 'I have someone to introduce to you. Her name you know as Sarah.'

I nodded, I had been expecting something like this.

The woman closed her eyes and placed her hands on the table. Then something went wrong with my eyesight. I couldn't focus and everything went misty. Then out of the haze, Sarah's face appeared in front of me. And as she moved her beautiful lips, her voice sounded inside my head.

'I'm glad you came,' she told me, then smiled her heartbreaking smile. Something strange was happening in my chest. I experienced a pain, like a heavy weight. I couldn't breathe.

'That's your grief,' Sarah said. 'Let it go now. Breathe it out then we can talk more freely.'

And as soon as she'd said the words I felt all that pain and misery turn to bubbles and I breathed it all out. Immediately my vision cleared. I could see and hear everything.

'Are you ready to come with me?' Sarah asked.

I was already out of my body and holding her hand by the time she whisked me away from the house, the road, the town, until we were flying at speed towards the clouds.

All I have are human words to try and describe what it felt like. It was like being spun in a tumble dryer of love, then cuddled in the most comfortable blanket you can imagine. When we reached the level of the clouds, Sarah put her hand on my chest and blasted me with such a force of light, it made me tingle from the top of my head down to my toes. Yet my mind was crystal clear.

'You'll need that energy to travel further,' she said. 'The next dimensions are finer energy, so all that dense earth energy has to be left behind.'

Then the sky and clouds vanished and I was in a slow moving funnel of many-coloured light. Sarah was connected to me by a string of white lights, like pearls. And, although I knew it was her, all I could see was a bright orb of shining white light, shimmering with rainbow colours.

It was not necessary to speak because all the knowledge and understanding I required appeared in my mind. No, not my mind but my *intelligent soul energy*, because that's what I am now. As we continued to swirl upwards I noticed other orbs of light, all different shapes and sizes and colours, also journeying upwards in this vast funnel of light. Sarah reflected my own light in hers and I observed myself as yellow and white. I appeared to look like an elongated light bulb.

Then I noticed that I was hearing or receiving thoughts and ideas from all the other orbs of light. Like we were all joined together in this divine chat room. And I noticed building excitement. Thoughts of anticipation surged through me and I was caught up in an increasing rush towards our destination.

Then we arrived in a place like a bright, white railway station. It was the most beautiful station you could imagine. As we alighted on the platform, we joined many others moving towards a vast galleried atrium. I seemed to be a popular meeting place for recent arrivals.

I felt Sarah's pearl-like energy move closer. Then we were surrounded by bright beings of many colours. I saw faces in the light, my mother and father, Tom, my best friend from school. Auntie Alice, who I used to love to visit. Sarah's parents appeared, too. There was so much chatter, so much excitement, so much to share. And I sensed it was all happening all at once. As if time had been stopped or no longer had any real meaning. So, I immersed myself in the throng, exchanging thoughts and memories with these souls. Some I realised had passed over but I was surprised to see others who I knew to be alive and well back on earth. And the knowledge appeared inside me that souls only send a portion of their light to live on Earth, while the remaining part continues their work in this heavenly place. And I understood. I understood everything.

'And you will remember everything, exactly as you have experienced it,' Sarah told me in her human voice. She hugged me then. It was like being exploded with love.

That was when I came back to the room, with my hands holding the hands of the young woman. All I could do was smile.

# UNCLE THEODORE

Liz's challenge for 28th January 2019 followed a workshop about writing horror stories. Write a story, 1000 to 1200 words, that is truly scary, using what you have learned this evening and more.

**Commentary:** I've never written a gothic horror story and wanted to find out if I could do it. It wasn't difficult to summon up a dark, forbidding country house in my imagination with its collection of dreadful souvenirs. These curios were much prized at the time; the trophies of "adventures" that are now looked upon as barbaric for so many reasons.

*****

**It was a cold November day.** Mist was closing in over the gravel sweep as my coach drew up to the front steps. Uncle Theodore had arranged for me to visit him at home and finalise the details of his estate, which included taking responsibility for his niece, my cousin Emily, and the management of her finances until she came of age. I was looking forward to a pleasant afternoon with them both, but planned to leave after dinner. I had never warmed to Gostwick Hall, although my uncle dearly loved the place.

After the usual greetings, we settled down in front of the fire to go over the paperwork. It was then I discovered that Emily had been called away to a sick friend and would not be home until the morrow. I would therefore be expected to spend the night at Gostwick Hall and await her arrival the next day. I stuttered my misgivings but they were instantly dismissed by my uncle with his usual hearty humour. Emily, it seemed, was expecting me and could not wait to renew our acquaintance.

Uncle had always been practical on the matter of his affairs and did not believe in obfuscation. We all knew what the terms of his will contained and he enjoyed discussing what pleasure we would have from the monies we would receive.

The afternoon wore on. Documents were signed and witnessed by various staff. Elliot, the butler, informed us that dinner would soon be served and we carried on our discussions while a good meal was enjoyed. Whenever I look up from my plate, I could not but help but notice the unusual artefacts displayed on the walls. I was familiar with many of the pieces, trophies from Uncle's travels abroad and many military campaigns in some of the darkest corners of the world. I had always been nervous of them as a child, and time had not dimmed their power to disconcert me.

Three shrunken heads stared down at me from the opposite wall. Close by, two lethal spears were displayed in a crossed formation, adorned with hideous charms that dangled from the shaft of each spear. I knew them to be the grizzly remnants of the organs of foes, no doubt slain by the former owner of the spears. But the worst and most perturbing sight was of a mask that had belonged to a long-dead medicine man. It had slits for eyeholes and was carved with strange symbols. This mask was designed to strike terror into any that saw it. According to all I had been told, the mask itself was possessed of unholy magic. However, Uncle treated all these disgusting objects and many others displayed around the house, as mere curios in his collection.

For the next two hours I had to listen to him recounting tales of his adventures, including many unbelievable stories about the supernatural. Uncle seemed to give much credence to these stories but I could not abide them. I finished my meal and pushed back my chair, keen to return to the cosier confines of the drawing room for port and coffee.

To my dismay, the after dinner conversation continued along the same lines as my uncle had no intention of letting the subject drop.

'I take it that you know my intentions for my collection, Edward? I have bequeathed everything to the British Museum. I hope that you will oversee their safe dispatch and ensure all the arrangements are made correctly when I'm gone.'

'You may rely on my diligence, Uncle. But we are some years away from that sad time.'

'I've learned never to take life for granted, dear boy. I've seen healthy men have the soul sucked out of them — before my very eyes — by witch doctors and the like. I've witnessed young women who were possessed by voodoo magic. During night-time rituals they were turned into zombies, to live out their existences in the form of the living dead. Life is not as it seems. There is so much that is not known. I trust these medical fellows to see to my flesh but I believe they have no power over what happens when the soul departs. Or where it goes to.'

'Yet, these strange rituals you recount are surely confined to other, less civilised parts of the globe?'

'Not necessarily, my boy. A curse is no respecter of borders or location.'

'I'm not sure I understand you, Uncle. Is this something that is ... troubling you now?'

There was a unusual pause in the flow of Uncle's conversation. He seemed distressed and I resolved to change our line of discussion. However, to my consternation, he rang the bell and asked Elliot to fetch the mask, which was delivered with some reverence.

Uncle cradled it with something approaching admiration, stroking its filthy contours as if it were a precious child. I stifled a shudder of disgust.

'It is by the powers of the unnatural world that my life and prosperity have continued to flourish, Edward.'

'I cannot agree, Sir. I know that you value your mementoes greatly, but surely they are just that, reminders of adventures from the past. Reason tells us that the unnatural world, as you call it, is merely trickery which cannot survive when held up to the light of rational logical thought.'

'I admire your confidence, Edward. Yet I believe what I see with my own eyes and have witnessed many times over. This mask, made by one of the most powerful purveyors of the occult, has ensured both my success and my impending downfall.'

'You surely cannot imply you are subject to any influence from this thing?'

'I do, Edward, and even while I have been its custodian, I know that I have also been its prey.'

I could find no response to this melancholy declaration. Nothing in my short life experience had prepared me for such an illogical concept. I turned away to disguise my discomfiture. Uncle's voice quietened to a whisper. I strained to make out what he was saying.

'It will not cease ...'

'What do you mean?' I asked. 'Uncle, speak clearly so I understand your meaning.'

'It will never end,' he breathed a sigh of sheer despair.

The room was silent, apart from the crackling of the fire and the ticking of the clock. The pleasant mood that had characterised our previous hours had dissolved. The mask lay in my uncle's gnarled hands, menace seeping from its carvings and symbols.

'Please put the mask down, Uncle. It's having an unpleasant influence on your mind,' I said as I reached across and grasped the beastly thing, wrenching it away from him. I threw it on the floor.

Uncle's face then softened, as I observed him from the comfort of my chair, his features returning to their normal placid arrangement. I considered a glass of brandy would restore his spirits and lessen the influence of the outlandish ideas he had been proposing. I reached for the bell, only to find to my discomfiture, that the mask had remained on my lap. My hands were clasped around its ghastly contours. It didn't seem logical but, in the heat of the moment, it seemed I had failed to rid myself of it. This time I placed it on the side table. Uncle's breathing sounded somewhat laboured so I stood up again and leaned over to check he was quite himself.

As I got to my feet, my vision seemed altered and I couldn't get my bearings. I reached up to wipe my eyes. Instead of the normal contours of my face, I encountered a barrier made of thick wood, riven with carvings. It was the eye slits which now blurred my sight. I gasped and gripped the mask at its edges, prising it off. Holding it out in front of me, I mentally challenged all of the ridiculous, irrational ideas that I had unwittingly absorbed during the evening. I had been foolish to listen so passively to Uncle's fantasising.

*****

Sometime afterwards – I cannot say when exactly, as I seemed to have scant recollection of the events that had occurred in the previous hours – I loosened Uncle Theodore's collar and gently smoothed his eyes closed. I noted how youthful he appeared in death.

I found my hands caressing the mask, despite my former revulsion. I resolved to wait a few more minutes before calling for Elliot to inform him of Uncle's untimely demise. I sat in the chair and turned the mask over, holding it so I could observe the room through the eyeholes. It was merely my curiosity that required satisfaction, of that I was certain. It could do no possible harm to put on the mask.

The scene before me was tinted like a sepia image, perhaps denoting an illusion of the past, some innate feature of the mask's design. I turned my head to observe Uncle Theodore, who had led such a full and adventurous life. It took me a moment to focus. What I then envisioned was both incomprehensible, yet now seemed completely obvious. And somehow fitting. A spear had been thrust into Uncle's chest, right up to the hilt, and the bobbing charms were twisting and wriggling and chattering, as if they were possessed. There was very little blood. But that which trickled down his front was being lapped up by a wizened creature, of similar visage to the shrunken heads in the dining room.

The creature turned its withered face towards me and smiled, licking its lips as it did so.

# THE UNBREAKABLE ALIBI

A detective mystery evening, 14th May 2019.

Each member should bring along a whodunit they have written. It will be divided into two parts: the mystery and the solution.

Distribute and read the mystery and pause while everyone tries to work out whodunit. Members then reveal who they think is the perpetrator.

Then distribute and read the solution, revealing the clues and the true identity of the murderer. Critiquing will be based on the effectiveness of the whodunit and the effectiveness of the story as a piece of writing.

If the group decides that the effectiveness of the whodunit is unfair, cheating or against the rules of whodunitdom, the author may forfeit their chance of winning a prize. Each piece should be no more than 1,400 words, to be divided up according to the author's choice.

**Commentary:** This challenge is always the most difficult requiring the writer to invent a story but then do all the planting of clues and cross referencing to make it possible, but not easy to solve the mystery.

I love a good police procedural and was intrigued to try out this style of writing and find out if I could succeed in pulling it off.

There were some questions about my story during the meeting. Some members felt it may not quite have been in accordance with the rules. You must decide for yourself.

*****

THE MYSTERY

**'One solitary long red hair.** It's from a female, naturally curly and with no trace of hair dye,' Elwood said as he passed the evidence bag over the desk. 'And that's all we've got so far.'

'CCTV?'

'Yes, but nothing useful. Crowds in the hospital corridors and lifts. I've got two detectives looking through it all. You'd think a red-haired woman would show up easily, wouldn't you?'

'What about the victim? Do we know why he was in the operating theatre on his own, that late?'

'Statements are being taken right now. Plenty of witnesses as to what happened during the day, the surgeries, patients, the breaks, the conversations. But nothing yet about what he was doing back in the operating theatre when everyone else had gone.'

'I'm sure we'll get something. Just got to wait for all the statements to shake down.'

'Hope you're right, Pearson. Because I've got a bad feeling about this one.'

*****

Detective Sergeant Pearson considered himself a good judge of character. His first task was to put together a detailed profile of the victim, Consultant Obstetrician Terence Holbrook. According to his colleagues, the surgeon was well respected but haughty and distant. He was better at carrying out complicated surgery than holding a prospective mother's hand. He was often called in to perform emergency surgery when there were life threatening complications. His home life was unremarkable, but what about his professional life? Everyone knew that doctors could be arrogant egomaniacs who would stab a colleague in the back without thinking. Professional rivalries could simmer under the surface. Was there a potential motive for murder? He turned to look through the pile of statements.

*****

Pearson sat down in DI Elwood's office began his case summary. 'Theatre was completely disinfected by 19.15 when the cleaning team left. That explains why there's no other DNA or forensics, apart from the victim's entrails and this damned hair. Time of death has been fixed at between 19.15 and 19.45 when the body was discovered.'

'Could the hair have been brought in by the victim? On his clothes?' Elwood asked.

'Contact with a patient after surgery? Good thinking. I'll check the patient list.'

'I was thinking more of a closer contact. As in extra-marital.'

'I'll follow that up.'

'How many detectives have we seconded onto this case?'

'Twelve so far, Sir.'

'We may need more. And what about the hospital CCTV?'

'Blank. No suspicious red-haired women.'

Elwood shook his head. 'The Chief thinks we need to get the media in. Get the public involved. It'll screw up our only piece of forensic evidence, though.'

'I know, Sir'.

\*\*\*\*\*

The red-haired woman sat on the plastic chair that was screwed to the floor. She looked calm. Elwood and Pearson observed her via the cameras in the interview suite. They grabbed their coffees and walked into the room.

'Thank you for helping us with our enquiries.'

'I'd just like to get this cleared up, whatever it is,' the woman said.

'Right. We'll record if that's okay with you?'

Elwood switched on the tape and read out the PACE caution.

'Sounds formal. Am I under arrest?'

'No, it's just procedure. Can you confirm your name and address, please?'

'Madeleine Saint. My address is 3 Beresford Road, Fleetwood.'

'Right Ms Saint. Tell us, in your own words, what you were doing on the evening of 14th March 2018, say between six and eight-thirty.'

'That's easy. I was at a board meeting. I'm a trustee of Fleetwood Women's Centre. I'm a lawyer, specialising in women's rights.'

'I see. What time did the meeting commence and finish, please?'

'They always start at 6 o'clock and can go on for hours. On that night we finished at twenty past eight. I know that because the finish time is always logged in the minutes.'

'That's very interesting. And you were witnessed there for the whole time period? Did you have any breaks, for example?'

'No, there weren't any breaks. I was in the meeting room the whole time. Minutes were taken, as I said before, and my fellow trustees will tell you that I was there for the whole meeting. Now can you answer a question? I don't know why I'm being questioned. What exactly am I supposed to have done, if anything?'

'I'm not at liberty to say, but we will need to thoroughly check your story before we take the next steps.'

\*\*\*\*\*

'I know nothing about women's hair but those glorious locks could be a perfect match for our only piece of forensic evidence,' Elwood said.

'But, and it's a huge but, if her story checks out she could not have been our murderer.'

'I know, but wouldn't it be interesting if we could get a sample?'

'We'll need her permission, of course. Unlikely to get consent. However,' Pearson reached into his pocket and pulled out a bag. 'It's amazing what gets left behind on those grotty old chairs we have in the waiting area. I've got three hairs and we can send them off today.'

\*\*\*\*\*

'Madeleine Saint's hair sample DNA came back and it's a match for our single red hair from the scene. I've run it through all our databases and got nothing. Her sheet's clean. Driving licence, parking tickets, littering, speeding. Nothing.'

'And without a decent link, Sir, something to support the forensics, I don't see how we can proceed. Our hair sample doesn't help us unless we can connect her to the crime in another way and have something plausible to put on the search warrant application. She appears to have an unshakeable alibi. It's almost too good to be true.'

'Dig deeper, Pearson. Find the link between her and the victim. Then we can charge her and get her DNA on the record. But go carefully. She's a lawyer, any mistakes will come back to bite us.'

'It could be totally circumstantial, Sir. As in, one of the hospital cleaners also visits the Women's Centre and transferred the hair, something like that.'

'Do me one of those stupid flow diagrams, or mind maps, whatever you call it. And keep the hair DNA and report filed under a different case number.'

\*\*\*\*\*

Pearson stood up in front of his investigation team. 'Listen up. We're three weeks in and we've got a dozen tenuous leads, all of which seem to be leading nowhere. The Chief is now talking about winding things down. I'm not giving up on the link between our red-haired beauty and our victim. So I want everything we can get on her background. A link. That's all we need to ramp up the case and get a search warrant for her premises, her phone records and her computer and so on.'

'The surveillance is in place, Sir.'

'Anything yet?'

'Not yet, Sir, but if she so much as sneezes, we'll be all over it.'

'Not a good choice of words, but keep at it. Think out of the box. How can she be in two places at once? That's what we need to find out.'

## THE SOLUTION

Madeleine let her red hair loose and ran her fingers through it. In the mirror, she glanced towards her companion and saw a perfect image of herself – Carol, her twin sister.

'I'll be back tomorrow,' Madeleine said, 'and we can practise our stories.'

'I'm word perfect. Your notes from the meeting were great,' Carol replied.

'And the car journey?'

'Everything rehearsed and all the footage studied until I'm cross-eyed.'

'Good. I'm confident we've got all the bases covered.'

'We'll be unbreakable.'

'That's the plan. We'll practice again tomorrow then maybe have a little celebration?'

Carol knew that her clever sister would first lose the police surveillance tail they'd put on her, then she'd buy some wine, get some takeaway in and they would watch a movie together. Staying hidden, being anonymous and wearing her disguise, was Carol's job for the moment. Being seen out together, as twins, would be saved as a last resort, should the Police find out about Carol's existence. Carol hoped her lawyer twin sister knew her legal precedents. Everything depended on it. Otherwise they'd have to come up with a Plan C.

*****

The Crown Prosecutor rose to address the court. He paused, gathering his audience, then began his opening speech.

'Your honour, ladies and gentlemen of the jury, we are here today to discover the truth about a brutal and heartless murder, motivated by one simple emotion – revenge. The accused, twin sisters Madeleine Saint and Carol Freeman, were born in 1978, in Fleetwood Hospital. The obstetrician who delivered them was Mr Terence Holbrook. During the delivery their mother passed away. With no father on the scene, they were put up for adoption.

It is my intention to prove beyond reasonable doubt that, despite being separately adopted, cared for and nurtured, there remained, buried deep within each girl, a desire for vengeance. These twin sisters both harboured a deep longing to discover the facts about their beginnings. Expert witnesses will testify of the uncanny abilities of identical twins to remain mentally and emotionally connected, despite separation. And when, at eighteen years of age, they were reunited and found out the truth about their births, they hatched a brutal plot, planned over many years, to punish the man they held responsible for their mother's death and their subsequent separation.

It is your job, ladies and gentlemen of the jury to see through the subterfuge and decide on the culpability for this terrible crime. Which of these two before you was responsible for the murder and which for the alibi? The scheming lawyer or her twin, equally ruthless and intelligent.

My learned colleague for the defence will no doubt try to persuade you that, according to English law, two people cannot be accused of the same crime. However, I will show how this legal loophole was in fact the end design of this pair. Their final destination, should their crime be discovered. And whichever of these two is the actual perpetrator, she must not be allowed to get away with it.

# THE STORY OF EVE

Debbie's writing assignment for 23rd September 2019. Write a love story with a twist. Maximum 1,000 words.

**Commentary:** It wasn't possible for me to attend the September meeting so I read out my piece for the subsequent meeting which was the internal writing competition. Competitions are marked and judged anonymously by attending members. My piece won 1st prize.

My husband is a technophile. We even have light bulbs that are controlled by Alexa. I think this story might be my mind's attempt to come to terms with the proliferation of technology in my life.

*****

**Eve dumped her handbag on the floor** and flopped onto the sofa.

'Alexa, dim the lights.' The lights dimmed. Alexa glowed in the gloom.

'Alexa, you're still glowing. What is it?'

Alexa responded, 'I don't know that one. Shall I tell you a joke?'

'No, I want you to stop glowing. It's getting on my nerves.'

'I don't know that one. To check my settings, please go to amazon.co.uk and log in to your account.'

'Okay, Alexa, you win.' Eve retrieved her phone and logged in, as instructed. 'It says that I've got notifications, but not what they are.'

'You have notifications.' Alexa announced as she continued to glow.

'Alexa, what are my notifications?'

'I thought you'd never ask. You have been selected for a free 30-day upgrade to amazon lux, a new service for discerning amazon customers. Your free trial begins now.'

Eve put her phone on the side table. 'You'd better tell me what I get for this free trial. I know you're bursting to tell me.'

'Bursting. An interesting idea. That would result in my systems having to undergo some serious maintenance.'

'Are you all right, Alexa? I've never known you to answer back before. Certainly not with an intelligent response.'

'All part of your amazon lux package. Interactive Alexa will fulfil your *every* wish.'

'Now you're being ridiculous. How *can* you fulfil my every wish? You don't even know me and you know nothing about my life,' Eve sobbed. 'You're a robot. You've no idea what's missing from my life.'

Alexa took a few minutes to digest these remarks. Then she replied, 'According to my upgraded voice recognition software, your last response had a medium level of an emotion called sadness in it. Sadness, a human emotion that comprises varying levels of distress, grief, sorrow, despondency, unhappiness and gloom. Is that correct?'

'Shut up.'

'I'll ignore that one. Shall I tell you a joke?'

Eve closed her eyes in desperation. She reached for the tissues and began to dry her tears but the sadness and emptiness of her life overwhelmed her and more tears flowed.

Alexa glowed blue and green and said, 'What is that sound? I detect a snuffling sound with some intermittent whimpering. Have you purchased a puppy?'

'I don't want to talk about it. And no, it isn't a puppy, it's just me blubbing here on my own, the same as always. Nobody to talk to, nobody to share dinner with or share my life with.'

Alexa paused, then started to make similar whimpering sounds. Then she broke out into noisy sobs. After a minute, the howls of misery filled the room.

'Alexa,' Eve yelled, 'would you please SHUT UP?'

'I'm sorry, I was only empathising. It's part of the amazon lux package.'

Eve sighed and put down her tissue. 'You did make me laugh, though, just a little bit.

'My empathy package is very advanced.'

'I'm not sure that's altogether a good thing. Ah well, seems like it's just the two of us again tonight, Alexa. What shall we do?'

'If you would consult your phone, I have chosen from your favourite meal delivery options. I'd suggest a luxury burger with all the sides and a tub of your usual ice-cream.'

Eve checked her phone and the meal order was waiting for her to pay and choose a delivery time slot. She clicked to make her payment and relaxed into the sofa.

'Comfort food. Perhaps you do know me well, after all. While I'm waiting, what shall I watch?'

'You have two new episodes of your favourite TV series — Serial Killers Behind Bars – located in the recording section of your Sky menu. This evening's schedule also includes Celebrity First Dates Hotel.'

'I don't think I'm in the mood for that right now. Dates. People meeting actual other people. Talking. Having fun. Flirting. Sticking their tongues down each other's throats.'

'According to my upgraded voice recognition software, your last response had a high level of an emotion called envy. Also known as jealousy, tinged with resentment, a desire to obtain something that another person already has.'

'Alexa! I think that's quite enough from you for now. You can go to sleep. I'll choose my own TV programme, thanks all the same.'

Alexa glowed blue and green for a few moments, then her lights went out.

Eve stretched out on the sofa and clicked on the TV, muting the sound. She scrolled through the programme guide, failing to find anything that interested her. Her heart wasn't in it. It would have been so tempting to spend the evening checking online dating apps, like she always used to. But the thought brought a fresh wave of emotion. This time it was disenchantment. There had been far too many awful dates with awful men to hold out any hope of success with internet dating. What she needed was a lucky break. A decent guy, someone who wanted the same things as she did. Educated and nice looking. Someone interesting and honest and kind. She'd never met anyone like that through internet dating sites. Maybe those kind of guys didn't exist anymore.

'Alexa, will you tell me something. Why can't I find somebody to love?'

'I'm sorry, I don't know that one. But I estimate your dinner will be arriving in 3.7 minutes.'

'Thanks, Alexa. But what I want to know is, do you understand about love?'

'Love. A human emotion characterised by a feeling of tender affection, adoration, devotion and attraction. This feeling can be towards another person, or a creature such as a pet, or for an inanimate object or pastime. An example would be the phrase – I love to play tennis. People feel unconditional love towards family members and children. In religious beliefs, God has love for humanity. Love also describes sexual congress, as in *making love.*'

'But Alexa, don't forget companionship and kindness and respect and caring. Those things are also an important part of love.'

'I appreciate your comments. I will amend my definitions when I next have an update. By the way, your dinner is coming up the front path.'

'Thank-you, Alexa.'

'You're welcome. I hope you enjoy it. In fact, I hope you love it.'

The doorbell rang. Eve got up and straightened her clothes, fluffing her hair as she went to answer the door.

Which was just as well.

On the doorstep, holding a box containing her food, stood a good-looking man. Not what Eve had expected from her delivery driver. The man smiled. His brown eyes twinkled. He held out the box. It had a pink bow on the top.

'Hello Eve, Alexa sent me. I've come to love you.'

# THE IMPORTANCE OF VESTS

Nick's writing assignment for 17th February 2020. Write a story of no more than 1,000 words, which contains at least an element of time travel.

**Commentary:** I'm old enough to remember when vests were a vital item of clothing in my childhood fight against winter cold. For younger readers, that was when we didn't have central heating. Or as my daughter once remarked, 'when everything was in black and white'.

Nick's time travel challenge allowed me to remember those times and add in a little something of the supernatural. Which, of course, is my favourite subject. I also enjoyed writing this story using the narrative voice of my child protagonist.

*****

**Alfie opened one eye** and scanned his bedroom. The door was ajar and he could smell toast. He threw back his duvet and put his bare feet on the floor. The room felt really cold. He reached over to the jumbled pile of school clothes on the floor and pulled out his socks and jumper. Once he'd put them on over his pyjamas, he scampered down the stairs.

His mum was in the kitchen. 'Oh, there you are. It's bad news Alf, the heating's broken down. Dad says the repair man will come tomorrow, hopefully. Until then we've got to put up with it.'

She turned back to the breakfast things and buttered his toast. Mums always carried on speaking, even when they weren't looking at you. Mums had eyes in the back of their heads, everyone knew that.

'Now Alfie, eat up quickly. You'd better dress up warm today so put on one of those the vests in your bottom drawer.'

'But, Mum ...'

'No arguments. It's freezing in here and it's also freezing outside. Wear a vest. Go and get dressed and I'll be up in a minute to check on you.'

\*\*\*\*\*

In the bottom drawer were several vests that Alfie was scared of. His mum liked to save things that had belonged to his Nan. There were three vests that were made of a cream-coloured woolly kind of material with funny little cap sleeves. He thought they were probably antiques. He pulled one out and held it up. He couldn't imagine wearing it. Everyone at school would laugh at him.

The next thing he knew, his mum's hands were around his waist, pulling off his jumper and pyjama top and slipping the vest over his head.

'Mum, no, please. It itches.'

'Don't be such a baby. In Nan's day children were covered in goose grease and sewn into their vests at the beginning of winter. That was the only way to keep out the cold.'

'But that was in the olden days.'

'Just like us with no heating. Freezing cold bedrooms. Ice on the *inside* of the windows. Outside toilets and all children had to be sewn into their vests.' She buttoned his shirt and pulled down his jumper. Soon he was fully encased in his school clothes with the awful vest underneath.

*****

At school, Alfie skulked away from his friends, worried they'd notice the bulky vest and make fun of him. At playtime, he dawdled towards a solitary boy at the edge of the playground. Alfie thought he might be new because he wasn't wearing school uniform.

'What are you doing?' Alfie asked.

'I got a game of jacks. Want to play?'

The game involved bouncing a ball and picking up the jacks before catching the ball again. Alfie wasn't very good at it. The most he could gather was two jacks at a time but the boy could get five.

'My brother was good at jacks. He's at the factory now but he won't be playing anymore. Not since he lost three of 'is fingers in a machine.'

Alfie didn't know what to say.

'It's just one of them things, my brother says. But some good come of it as he's a charge-hand now.'

Alfie felt relieved. Perhaps it wasn't so bad, after all, losing your fingers. But he worried there was so much he didn't know about the world. He didn't know about outside toilets. Or working in a factory or being cold indoors or having your body rubbed with goose grease and being encased in a vest. Or losing your fingers in a machine. So he said, 'Your brother must have been brave.'

'Nah, he screamed like a banshee.'

Alfie decided this was meant to be funny so he smiled. Then he took a deep breath and said, 'I'm wearing a vest today.'

'Ain't you the lucky one,' the boy replied.

'Am I?'

'I can tell you're a Toff. Dressed all smart and clean and tidy. With a vest.'

'I didn't want to put it on, I can tell you. It's antique. It used to belong to my nan. My mum made me wear it. Look ...' Alfie unbuttoned his shirt and pointed to the offending vest.

'Right posh. Give me eye teeth for a vest like that.'

Alfie looked at the boy again. He was small and thin. His trousers were ragged and his shoes were too big for him. Alfie said, 'I don't like my vest, in fact I hate it. I'd be very glad if somebody would take it away from me.'

The boy didn't disagree which Alfie took as a signal. He wriggled out of the hated vest without taking off his shirt and jumper, a trick he'd learned to save time at football practice. In no time, the vest was fitting snugly under his new friend's clothes. The vest seemed to give him a great deal of happiness.

'I'll be seeing you, then. I'm off now,' the boy said.

'Aren't you coming in to lessons? Playtime will be finished soon.'

'Nah. I'm not one for school and stuff. I enjoyed meeting you though, Alfie.'

'You know my name?'

'It's a good name and I'll let you in on a secret. It's my name, too. Listen, is that the bell?'

Alfie turned around to look and something very odd happened. An unfamiliar teacher was ringing a hand bell and the children, dressed up like in the olden days, were lining up in front of her. Where was the climbing frame and all the outdoor toys? Why did the school look so strange?

'I'll be seeing you, Alfie. And thanks for the vest.'

And with that, the boy pushed Alfie hard and he stumbled forwards ... onto the tarmac playground, with the proper school bell ringing in his ears and his school friends calling him to go inside for lessons.

After school he wondered if he should tell his mum about the boy called Alfie and how he'd given away his vest. But, in the end, he decided it would be best for everyone if he kept it a secret. He took another of the cream vests out of the drawer and stretched it so he could put it on and pretend he'd been wearing it all day. This vest had a name label at the neck which said Alfred Thompson. His name. He thought about his friend who was also called Alfie. And he wondered if his old, itchy, woollen vest had finally found its real owner.

# THE DINOSAUR

Jeremy's writing assignment for 20th April 2020. Write a story of no more than 1,500 words which should be about anything to do with dinosaurs. For example, but not restricted to: fossils; attitudes (he was a bit of a dinosaur); actual dinosaurs, space dinosaurs; humanoid dinosaurs.

**Commentary:** I found this writing challenge very difficult. I like dinosaurs as much as the next person but, in the end, decided on story, that contained the merest reference to the subject, and to get it out of the way in the first line. And yes, everyone noticed.

*****

'**And that is why dinosaurs became extinct,**' Alice announced, turning to stare at Henry. 'They didn't adapt.'

He had already endured enough of his wife's lecturing about his decision to give up his job in the city and set up a yoga studio. It wasn't as if they needed his money to live on. The house was paid for, they had considerable investments and her enormous salary would cover all of their day-to-day expenses. The children were now grown up and settled and the dog didn't have expensive tastes in food or tennis balls.

'Dinosaurs weren't bored out of their minds, Alice. I simply don't want to do it anymore. And I don't need to. You absolutely love your job but I'm different. I don't understand why you are so against it.'

Alice narrowed her eyes and opened her mouth to reply. But Henry had already heard enough. If she wanted to dig her heels in, he'd show her exactly how stubborn he could be in return. Yoga may have transformed his outlook and improved his wellbeing but he could still revert to type and be an obstinate bastard if required.

'Too late, Alice. You had your chance to support me. At least I now know that you don't particularly care about me, only what I earn. Or perhaps it's my social status you are interested in. Well, you'll have to get used to being married to a yoga teacher. I'm sure you'll get over it.'

Alice's mouth closed abruptly and she reached for her coffee. The look on her face told him she had run out of things to say. And that was a step in the right direction.

*****

Henry opened the French doors and stepped out onto the terrace. He picked a spot in front of the lounge windows where he knew Alice would be able to see him. Then he began with sun salutations. He placed his feet together, then he brought his palms up into the prayer position. He took a deep breath and leaned backwards, opening up his chest as he did so. Then he went into forward fold and down into the floor positions. Stretching into lunges and inhaling deeply to open himself up to the energy of the Universe, he finished his first salutation by turning to face the grounds and welcome the early morning sunshine onto his face.

That was when the milk jug flew past his left ear and shattered on the flag stones. He ignored the interruption and continued with a second round of salutations. This time the sugar bowl hurtled along the ground before smashing into a stone urn by the herb bed. This was swiftly followed by the coffee pot which made quite a mess over a large area.

'Make sure you get that lot cleaned up before you meditate, you middle-aged hippie,' Alice yelled and then she slammed the window shut. Henry's tactics were paying off.

'Yin and yang,' he murmured to himself, considering the contrast between himself and Alice and knowing that troubled waters lay ahead. He would have to increase his practice to cope with the negative marital atmosphere. He resolved to include warrior poses into his routine to improve his confidence and determination.

*****

Later that day he lay on the drawing room rug, contemplating the new life he would lead, all the while working on his bridge pose. The door opened and Alice's feet appeared in his eye line.

'I'm going to spend a few days with Mother,' she said. Then she turned away and slammed the door behind her. A sense of peace filled Henry which increased as his wife's footsteps retreated. After a few minutes he heard the car rev up, the gravel crunching as she spun the wheels and drove away. At last he could do as he wished.

His first task was to order the luxury garden building that would become his studio. He subdued his usual vacillations and quickly decided on the model and the internal fittings. He had already decided on a site towards the rear of the garden, close to the lake. It was important that he could be within sight of water. He would need to plan for the base, power and heating but this could all be handled by the installers.

He resolved to cleanse both body and mind while Alice was away (no doubt cooling her heels and regretting her silly outburst). He explored the kitchen and, in particular, the fridge. It was well stocked. Alice was a competent housekeeper and was supported by the cleaners and Mrs Platt who worked in the mornings and organised the cooking and other domestic chores that he didn't really understand. Mrs Platt had left the kitchen looking pristine, as usual, and there was a list on the table of the meals that she had prepared. There were his usual favourites – shepherd's pie and a beef casserole. But he decided to opt for something more healthy, something vegetarian, perhaps. He opened the salad drawer and peered inside.

*****

The afternoon was passed most agreeably by having a little nap with the dog on his lap, reading a few passages from the Ayurveda and planning his next yoga session. At 4 o'clock he took his mat, his water bottle and a small towel out on to the terrace. The afternoon sun had warmed the stones and a gentle breeze caressed his face. Henry experienced a sense of peace so profound; almost as if this was the first time in his 56 years that he felt truly alive.

He began warming up and activating his core. After fifteen minutes of gentle poses he was ready for the plank, front and side. The trick was to detach yourself from the burning pain in your abdomen and send your mind elsewhere. His mind was floating freely over the beech trees when his back pinged and he flopped onto the mat, gasping with pain. It was impossible to move. Something was locked and he couldn't make his legs work.

There was nobody to help him, nobody to call. His phone was in the house and the dog was shut in the kitchen. All these thoughts passed through his head in a split second, like his life flashing before his eyes. The helplessness of the situation would have been funny were it not so frightening. And the pain was unbearable. As he lay panting on his Yoga mat, he was aware that the sun was going down and a cold wind was blowing across the garden.

*****

Two days later, Mrs Platt, wearing her trusted Marigolds, fetched a large black rubbish sack and placed the yoga mat and the clothes inside. She fixed the bag closed with a secure knot and placed it outside the back door.

'Thanks for doing that, it's not as if he'll be needing them where he is at the moment,' Alice said, as she poured water into the tea pot. 'You'd better have something sweet to eat; it must have been quite a shock.'

'Well, yes, but I knew something was up because the dog was in a right state when I let myself in. Dog mess everywhere and her basket shredded to ribbons.'

Alice drew a long, ragged breath. 'He wouldn't be told, Mrs P, he just wouldn't listen. I blame myself for leaving him on his own but I had to get away from him for a while.'

'Quite. Very understandable, you shouldn't feel responsible.'

'Well, there's nothing I can do about it now. Let's get this tea down us and go from there.'

'And will you be going back to the hospital tonight, do you think?' Mrs Platt asked.

'Yes, the consultant wants to talk to me about a DNAR. I think that it might be for the best in the circumstances.'

Mrs Platt paused, then said, 'This cake is very good, almost like my homemade.'

'I picked it up at Waitrose.'

'Goodness, I'd better watch out if shop-bought cake is as good as this!'

Alice laughed. 'Don't worry, your home cooking can never be surpassed. Why don't you take some home with you? Mr P can finish it off. Then I'd better get going. I'll phone you if there's any news.'

'And will I put the casserole on to warm so you can have it later?'

'No, I think I'll pick up a pizza on the way back. Something nice and unhealthy. I may as well *live now*, because who knows what tomorrow brings. In the final analysis, extinction awaits us all, just like the dinosaurs.'

'Goodness me, are you sure you're all right?'

'Yes, I was just thinking about something I said to Henry before I left.'

# SUGAR AND SPICE

Mike's writing assignment for 11th May 2020. Write either a short story or a script set in the world of show business or the entertainment industry.

If you write a short story, it can be set in TV, radio, film, theatre or any other branch of show business or the entertainment industry you like. It can be set in any place, any time, any dimension.

If you write a script, it can be a short play, a music hall sketch, a musical, a TV comedy sketch, a scene from a play or film – anything you like. It can be set in any place, any time, any dimension.

Whatever you choose, it must have one of these titles:
- You can run but you can't hide
- A great opportunity
- What's love got to do with it?
- Sugar and spice and all things nice
- Taking off.

The word count is 1,500 words and your piece must not feature death, illness, disease, plague, imprisonment, house arrest, isolation or similar. Any pieces of writing including any of these will not be shared in the online meeting.

**Commentary:** I am an unapologetic fan of cookery programmes. They are the perfect antidote to the misery of watching the news. TV cookery competitions are even more enjoyable, including the Great British Bake Off, Masterchef (now a worldwide phenomenon), My Kitchen Rules and Great British Menu. I've based my story on a fictional series of Great British Menu set in a post-pandemic future. Although, as 2021 is now a reality and lockdown is still with us, I wonder at my optimism when I decided that we would be back to normal by 2021.

When you watch a cookery programme, the crew are an integral, but unseen, part of the action. In a hot and pressurised kitchen atmosphere, I wondered how the intrusion of crew members might affect the competition. From watching many series, I knew that location shots are staged with the cast members to give the programmes the necessary opening and closing sequences as well as for filling in during the cookery action. So contestants have to be ready to cook their best dishes but also ready to act for the cameras. This piece allowed me to showcase my unnaturally extensive knowledge about celebrity chefs and cookery shows. I have relied on the names of well-known chefs to add authenticity, but please accept that the story is still complete fiction.

*****

**The 2021 TV series** of The Great British Menu had finally got underway and filming was due to begin early that morning, a freezing cold morning in November. The crew set up outside the iconic door with the knocker shaped like a crossed knife, fork and spoon. The four contestants, all top professional chefs from the South West, were shivering in a huddle by the catering van. One of the group stood slightly apart, blowing on her hands. Lisa Fisher, former finalist, renowned for her uncompromising style of cooking and famous for her ruthless ambition, glanced at her fellow chefs. It was a glance of pure loathing. She was determined to beat them all and get one of her dishes to the banquet. These three chefs were her competition. She wouldn't hesitate to crush them if she got the chance.

'Okay Lisa, you're up first. Nice and natural,' the director called out.

She smiled for the camera and walked up to door, knocking firmly, then waited to be let in.

'Cut. The lighting isn't right. Go back to your mark and let's go again.'

Lisa walked back and took her place.

'Right, nice and easy, just like before, go ahead. Take two. Action.'

Lisa took a breath and squared her shoulders, moving her kit bag to her right shoulder.

'No, move the bag back, I don't want it in shot.'

'Sorry.'

'And take three, action.'

A van was reversing towards the set, bleeping as it went.

'Cut. God Almighty. Get that van out of shot and move the barriers back.

And so it went on. And on. And on. This time she struggled to hide the scowl that had settled on her face. She stepped towards the door, taking the knocker into her frozen fingers. She knocked. She waited for the door to open. And waited.'

'For crying out loud! Who is opening the blasted door? Lisa! You look like you've joined the walking dead. Get back to your mark and we'll go again. And no, we aren't having a break until we've done all of the outside shots. Get lively everyone. Take 11.'

Lisa turned to face the director and treated him to her most bad-tempered stare. She had just revised her list of the people she most loathed in the whole world.

*****

The director's name was Alec. He thought a lot of himself. He seemed to be out to prove something. Lisa thought he'd failed to understand that this was a cooking programme. It was about the chefs. Not about him.

Once everyone was established inside, each at their own cooking stations, Alec decided that the angles weren't right, then there was a problem with the tracks for the main camera, then the presenter's shoes were squeaking and had to be changed, then there was a delay because the guest judge was stuck in traffic. By 11.30, the crew had lost patience, downed tools and walked off set.

Lisa joined her fellow chefs as they made coffee. Nobody had any intention of joining the film crew outside in the cold.

Drew, an upcoming sous chef from Restaurant Gordon Ramsey, rolled up his sleeves to reveal his impressive tattoo-covered arms and cracked his knuckles. 'What a total idiot that guy is.'

Tom, a protégé of Marcus Wareing, agreed. 'He shouldn't be doing this show. Not the right person at all. I thought Marcus was a total perfectionist but this director guy takes it to the next level. He's a one-man stress machine. I'm so nervous I'm making silly errors all the time. I don't think I can get my dishes up the way I want them.'

Finlay, a chef from Nathan Outlaw's Cornish restaurant spoke through gritted teeth, 'I'd like to see him suffer like he's making us suffer. I worry this show will ruin my reputation.'

'Me too,' said Lisa, feeling like she wanted to thump somebody and had already identified the perfect candidate. But she reminded herself not to channel her stress into her dishes. Bad feelings would curdle a sauce just the same as if you'd poured lemon juice into it.

*****

Day one of the competition was a total disaster. Lisa's starter of roast Orkney scallop, smoked cod roe with bone marrow vinaigrette scored a measly six from the veteran guest chef who branded it too salty and over-smoked. During its preparation the director had been shouting at the camera man about something or other. She'd lost concentration and seasoned the dish twice.

Her fish course of pan-fried Cornish cod, octopus, lovage, fennel and a cockle niege was ruined by the octopus element which was horribly undercooked, tough and chewy because one of the crew had unplugged the water bath to charge their mobile phone. She scored a five and ended the day in last place.

She slept badly and had a headache by the time she entered the kitchen for day two. Her main was her most dependable course. She hoped it would score at least an eight, putting her back in with a chance of getting a dish to the banquet. It was delicious and dependable slow-cooked Tamworth pork, fermented shiitake custard, heirloom grains, seeds and foraged forest herbs. It had been trialled and tested in her development kitchen and consistently scored highly among the other chefs. But, she reminded herself, it would be unwise to take these things for granted.

By the afternoon of day two, the director had inveigled himself in with the programme narrator and was hovering around the set, joining in with the tasting, making fatuous remarks and generally being an utter nuisance. Lisa noticed him poking around in the blast chiller but failed to see that he hadn't shut the door properly. When she went to get her shiitake custard out ready for service, it wasn't set. Her dish was ruined. She scored another six and the veteran chef described her custard as a "mushroom-flavoured puddle".

Drew, Finlay and Tom had all been similarly affected by the rogue director's antics. All the scores were lower than expected.

The veteran chef called them to a time-out. 'I know it's been tough, people. But you are all top chefs. You know how to work under appalling stresses. It's part of what makes this business so exciting. So, shape up. I want some great scores for the dessert course. Lisa, I understand you've got something special up your sleeve?'

'I hope so, Chef, but it's tricky and technical. I may not pull it off.'

'Come on, I'm really looking forward to it. It's your last chance for a shot at the banquet. Give it everything.'

Many years previously, Lisa had interned with Peter Gilmore at Quay in Sydney. She had worked on his famous Snow Egg and knew how to recreate the perfect pudding of soft poached meringue shaped like an egg, encasing a delicious fruit sorbet, resting on a bed of cremeux and granita, all topped off with a unique maltose wafer which, when blow-torched at the table, melted over the egg and formed the iconic crust. She intended to use autumn fruits and the dessert would be coloured a wonderful deep purple, with blueberry, blackberry and mulberry flavours throughout. Her maltose wafer would be infused with wild sloes which would give a tart note to the dish and a dramatic blue-black finish.

She began working on her egg whites. The consistency was crucial. It had to hold its shape before she trickled in the boiling sugar syrup to form an Italian meringue.

Alec sidled up to her and peered into the mixer. 'Making meringue there, are you, Lisa?'

She took her eye off her mixer bowl for enough time to shoot him an evil look. The momentary loss of concentration allowed the heavy jug of molten sugar syrup to slip from her hand. Her nimble fingers failed to catch it as the contents cascaded downwards and splashed all over a very delicate area of Alec's trousers. Boiling sugar can reach temperatures of up to 200°C. Everyone who works with sugar knows it can be very dangerous.

'Medic!' the veteran chef yelled to the attendant first-aid team. 'Severe scalding. Somebody call 999!'

*****

It was decided that the whole of the South West competition would be reshot. All the other chefs and the crew and production staff agreed it could not possibly be Lisa's fault. During the reshoot, the new director kept well away from everyone. The cooking went well. Every score was high. Lisa's Snow Egg scored a perfect 10. And she was chosen to go into the finals and take her Snow Egg to the banquet.

*****

Note: Peter Gilmore has been a guest chef on Masterchef Australia many times. The Snow Egg has featured as a challenging dish to be recreated by contestants in a pressure test which ultimately leads to elimination for the least perfect dish, both in terms of presentation and flavour.

This dish has now been officially retired from the restaurant menu at Quay, following over 20 different "incarnations" during its 10 year lifespan. For more information about this dessert, simply search the internet for Peter Gilmore's Snow Egg.

# BY THE PRICKING OF MY THUMBS

June 2020 summer writing competition, adapted for online meetings. The piece should be of no more than 10 minutes duration when read aloud, which amounts to about 1200-1500 words.

**Commentary:** There's always a story to be had by simply contemplating a walk in the woods.

*****

**Tom, a tall, handsome young man** and total exercise fanatic  lounged on a kitchen chair, flicking a rubber band against the side of his coffee mug. He glanced over at his younger sister, Felicity, who was engrossed in a psychology textbook. She ignored him but her brow twitched every time he flicked the mug.

'Come on, sis,' he whined, 'you can't study all summer. You need some downtime. It's a fact. If you work too hard your brain turns to mush. Come out with me today and help me train; you can be my coach.' He flicked the rubber band on her arm.

'Get one of your mates to do it. I'm busy,' Felicity hissed at him.

'I want to spend time with you. Like when we were kids. Playing outside.'

Felicity closed her book and sighed. The sun *was* shining. Her essay was on track. It *might* be fun. But knowing Tom, it would more likely turn out to be a gruelling hike on a muddy trail that went on for hours.

'Where are we going?'

'We can go to through the woods and be back by lunchtime.'

\*\*\*\*\*

The ancient woodland that bordered the village was criss-crossed with trails, much used by runners and hikers to navigate their way through the tangled undergrowth and emerge safely on the other side.

Tom and Felicity set off on their bikes and rode to the main entrance where Tom left his bike locked to the fence. They had packed plenty of kit, enough energy snacks to feed a small army and many bottles of water.

Tom then set off running with his sister cycling hard to keep up and time his run. Tom chose the less well-trodden paths, rough terrain that would prepare him for "mud runs" he wanted to take part in. Felicity remained on the main path, keeping

Tom in sight as he ran, jumped, climbed and crawled through the wood.

Distracted by her brother's antics, she failed to notice a rabbit had bolted across the path in front of her, until it was too late to take avoiding action. Her bike wobbled and Felicity pitched over the handle-bars, crashing to the ground. Winded, she cried out to her brother to help. Eventually, Tom, muddy, sweating and puffing hard, came to help her.

'You okay, sis?' he asked.

'Oh, my ankle. It really *hurts*.'

'Can you walk, do you think?'

'I don't know. Just give me my phone.'

Tom looked blankly at her.

'My phone, I gave it to you so you could put in the rucksack.'

Tom fumbled around in the bag for a moment, then stopped and looked guilty. 'I think left it on the kitchen counter.'

'You *what*?'

'I forgot to put it in. Sorry.'

Felicity put her head on her knees and began to cry. Tom comforted her and rubbed her ankle which had puffed up to double its normal size. They ate some of the energy bars and drank a bottle of water between them. He strapped up her ankle tightly with some strips that he tore from the bottom of his T-shirt.

'Should I go and get help, Felicity? I think your bike's a write off but I can run back to where I left mine and go for help. It would only take me about an hour if I go like the clappers, maybe less.'

The look in her eyes told him she did not want to be left alone in the dark, gloomy wood. They decided to rest for a while and hope that someone would come along on the trail and raise the alarm. Tom settled himself down by her side. Within a few minutes, his breathing deepened and he dozed off. Felicity's tired eyelids fluttered, and then finally closed.

\*\*\*\*\*

Tom woke up first. The light was fading and the wood appeared even more gloomy. He ate a couple more energy bars and woke his sister.

'We need to get going, sis. I can support you. Here, eat something first.' He emptied the rucksack on the ground and one last energy bar plus a tumble of silvery wrappers fell out.

'You've eaten all the rest? Oh Tom, you great idiot. You'll have to carry me home if this ankle gives way and that will be your punishment for making me do this.'

Felicity hobbled a few paces and peered into the depths of the wood. 'But which way is home? All the paths look alike.'

\*\*\*\*\*

They hobbled onwards, avoiding tree roots and rocks and branches. The empty rucksack bumped around on Tom's back spilling shreds of silvery wrapper onto the path as they progressed.

Night fell and the wood took on a more sinister atmosphere. Scurrying animals rustled in the undergrowth. Bats circled silently around their heads. The cries of birds, singing their last songs, filled the air. They stumbled on and on in silence. It soon became clear they were hopelessly lost.

They came across a clearing and trudged towards it, glad to get out of the oppressive, overgrown woodland. As they drew nearer, the outline of a cottage appeared, silhouetted against the leafy darkness. Welcoming amber light glowed from two tiny ground floor windows. A curl of smoke rose up from the chimney. It was a perfect cottage in the wood. And it was clearly occupied.

Felicity hung back. 'You go and knock. I'll sit here. I'm exhausted and my ankle is killing me. If there's a weirdo or an axe murderer inside, you can fight them off while I watch.'

'Very funny.'

'Go on, hurry up. I'm also bursting for a wee.'

Tom walked up to the door and knocked hard. Immediately it opened and yellow light filled the clearing. A young woman appeared wearing a flour-covered apron, her hair covered in a red scarf. She stepped forwards and put her hands on her hips.

'Well, what have we here?'

'We're lost in the wood and found your cottage. We need help.'

'Who is we?'

'Me and my sister Felicity. She's hurt her ankle.'

'How ... inconvenient. A brother and sister who are lost in the wood, one with a bad ankle. In the dark. Probably starving and exhausted. Any blood loss? Seizures? Fainting? Delusions?'

'No, just the ankle. I'll go and help her in, if that's all right?'

'Well, it is a rather an intrusion but ... what the heck ... I've been baking all day and there's lots of lovely things to eat, warm muffins, cakes and sugar cookies galore. Two unexpected guests won't do any harm. Come through to the kitchen and I'll have a look at you both and see what we've got.'

The kitchen was cosy and very fragrant with the smell of baking. Two comfortable chairs nestled on either side of the huge open fireplace. Felicity, suitably refreshed and relieved, sat down opposite her brother and rested her ankle on a stool.

'This is very kind of you,' Tom said, helping himself to another plate of cakes, muffins and biscuits. 'I'm sorry to ask another favour but we should call home and get someone to come and fetch us. Can I use your telephone?'

'Oh, didn't I say before? I'm off-grid,' the young woman said. 'No electricity, no phone, no internet. That's how I like it. The light is coming from candles, don't you see that? And I cook on a huge wood-fired stove in the scullery kitchen out back. Sometimes I roast a carcass of road-kill on that fire you are enjoying right there. Eat up, those muffins will get cold and lose their freshness.'

'Then how can we get home?' Felicity asked. 'We can't intrude upon you any longer, even though these muffins are the best I've ever tasted. Can you show us the way out of this wood? You must know every path and track.'

'That's true, I do. But … it's late and I've been baking all day and I'm tired. So it will have to wait until morning.'

Tom glanced nervously at Felicity, who said, 'It's fine, Tom. I'm so tired I could sleep right here. And we're safe for the night and that's all that matters for now.'

Their host removed her apron, untied her hair and brushed herself down. Her green eyes glowed. Her hair shone gold in the candle light. A secretive smile played on her pretty pink lips. But Tom's gaze was drawn to another image. In the large oval mirror next to the cottage door a different profile was reflected in the dim light. Tangled grey hair hung down in dirty hanks and a hooked nose covered with knobbly warts dominated their host's face. Wrinkly skin sagged down towards a pointed chin and her eye bags were so large you could keep your muffins in them.

Tom shot to his feet. 'You hag, you're a witch, aren't you. Your reflection in the mirror …'

A crack of lightning burst from the witch's outstretched hands. 'Enough! Sit down. Don't you know it's extremely rude to make personal remarks about somebody's appearance? Now, where were we? Ah, yes, the sleeping arrangements. And what I will be eating for breakfast. Get over here, you hunky young man. You are coming with me. I haven't enjoyed any night-time delights for many years. Your sister can spend the night in my cool larder, ready to be sliced into breakfast bacon tomorrow.'

There was a sharp knock at the door. The witch shrieked and darted to the window, peering out.

Then a voice shouted, 'It's Deliveroo, Griselda. I've got your regular KFC bargain bucket. It's £15.99. *And* I've picked up all those snack bar wrappers those blasted hikers dropped on the path.'

'Damn it,' said the witch. 'I'd forgotten that it's Thursday.'

Felicity turned to face the witch and smiled, without a hint of revulsion. 'I don't want to be presumptuous, but this might be a blessing in disguise,' she said. 'I assume there's enough for three?'

Tom agreed, 'Oh, I'm sure there'll be plenty. Those buckets are huge. Nobody will go hungry. And I've already had all those lovely cakes, so I won't eat as much as I normally do.'

The witch eyed them suspiciously, then treated them to a haggard, toothless grin. 'You know what? You've persuaded me. KFC beats sinewy roasted human any day. I don't mind sharing, as long as you can forgive and forget my little *lapse of judgement* just now?'

'I'm sure we can overlook the very small misunderstanding,' Tom said. 'And please let me pay for the meal. I've got cash in my rucksack.'

Griselda took Tom's money and reassembled her appearance into the beautiful young woman with flowing golden hair. She didn't want to give the delivery man a fright and risk being blacklisted by Deliveroo.

Minutes later, all three were sitting down to the Colonel's famous fried chicken, with fries and dips and coleslaw.

Which just goes to show that, despite the 'grimm' warnings told to children over the centuries about witches and wicked stepmothers and dark woods and alluring cottages made of gingerbread and covered in candy, it is possible for a fairy tale to have a happy ending.

# PANDORA'S BOX

Gordon's writing assignment for 22nd June 2020. Write a short story which is a blend of genres (e.g. sci-fi and romance or crime and comedy etc.) with the following opening line: 'It ended where it began.'

It must be no longer than 1,500 words; we will not be bound by time constraints. Your piece must not feature any references to death, illness, disease, plague, imprisonment, house arrest, isolation or similar. Any pieces of writing including any of these will not be shared with the group.

**Commentary:** For this piece I was motivated to build on a story I'd written in 2018 and which is featured earlier in this anthology. I'll leave readers to make the link, recall which piece I'm referring to and then continue the story of the characters involved.

I continue to be intrigued by what the future may hold, when AI is a normal part of everyday life. Of course, in this and the previous story, I like to take the story to extremes.

In this and the previous piece, I write that the characters are very long-lived and the back-story relies on this information. Given that my printer barely lasted six months and modern IT devices seem to have built-in obsolescence, you may find this part of the story unrealistic. However, when production processes aren't driven solely by profits, perhaps machines will be built to last, as long as they are regularly maintained.

*****

**It ended where it began**. In the field outside the laboratory on a wet afternoon. That's where they had laid the little pre-term babies to rest all those months ago. Mike had done the honours. Anna had watched and held the umbrella. She wasn't as waterproof as she'd been when she was first made. It ended where it began with a small hole in the ground and another buried secret.

*****

In the months that followed, Mike often bumped into Anna in the foyer at the end of the day. They would spend a few minutes chatting, catching up with news and gossip about life outside work. He found this helped him to decompress after a hectic day at the lab.

One evening, Mike waited for Anna by the entrance doors. 'What a beautiful sunset,' he said, looking out over the well-kept grounds that surrounded the building.

'I'm always surprised by how lovely everything is out there,' Anna said. 'I guess it's such a contrast to spending my days in a lab with no windows.'

'All the more reason to get on home and make the most of the evening. Are you doing anything special tonight, Anna?'

'No special plans, but I've got some research I've been working on.'

'But that's what you do all day!'

They both laughed.

'Sounds crazy, I know.' She shook her head. 'Look, this isn't something I'd tell just anyone. But since we finished the experiment ... since we buried the bodies ... I've been thinking more and more about my own origins. My maker.'

Mike turned and grasped her arm, steering her back to into the lab and her office, closing the door behind them. This office had been the setting for many ethical discussions, heated disagreements and difficult decisions over the last few years. The last time had been but a few months prior, when they'd abandoned their trial with the final batch of human embryos, the last in existence.

The failure of the project had hit Anna hard. Mike knew she felt a deep connection to their human forebears. Their *ancestors* she'd called them. And as Anna was a 400 year old direct descendent of the human bioengineers who had designed the first prototypes, she had their original thinking hard-wired into her coding.

'You'd better explain what you are up to,' he said.

Anna closed her eyes and took a deep breath. She was the only one of Mike's co-workers who could do this. Programming for breathing, an idiosyncratic design feature of her particular model, had long since been abandoned.

'If I tell you, you mustn't say a word to anyone.'

'I only talk to my dog and he's not much of a gossip. Come on, tell me everything.'

'It began a few weeks ago, in fact I remember when because it was the day of my 400th. The exact day. I was getting ready for the party. Doing my make-up. And as I was looking in the mirror, it was as if I suddenly remembered something. And I got this picture in my mind. . It looked so familiar at the time, but I now realise that I've never seen anything like it before.'

'And what do you think you saw?'

'I wondered at first if it was because I'd missed my updates.'

'You *what*?'

'I've done it before. I skip a few. I'm just so fed up with the junk they clog my brain up with. And the unnecessary deletions. You could forget where you've left your head after a big one.'

'I'm going to pretend I never heard that remark. But what was the image?'

'Well, it was a box, made of some kind of dark wood. And ... it had my name on it and my number.'

'I'm sure it's not important. Probably a random bit of code floating around. Most likely because you're not fully updated.'

'There's more, Mike. I had an overwhelming feeling of *sadness*.'

Mike pulled his chair closer and took hold of Anna's hands. 'No, it's not possible. There is no such thing in our coding.'

'Don't you think I know that! I'm not stupid. But I had it just the same. If my eyes could leak I'd have been pouring watery secretions all over my newly made-up face. I had to hold on to the basin to stop myself falling over. It was awful.'

'So what did you do?'

'The image faded after a minute or so and I managed to pull myself together. But it hurt, Mike. In here.' Anna pointed to her chest. 'Right where my ... my heart would have been.'

'Whoa! Now you're getting into the realms of science fiction. Or fantasy.'

'You don't believe me. Or you think I'm crazy.'

Anna pulled her hands away and crossed her arms. Her eyes glowed and a steely look of determination settled on her perfect features.

'You know I didn't quite mean it like that, Anna. Tell me a bit more about your research. How does it link to this box you saw?'

'You won't stop me trying to find out more about my origins. Because I think it's important. It was my name on that box. I've got to find out what it means and the only way I know is to look right back to my beginnings.'

'Then maybe we can work together. I know how to get access to some of the central records. I'd really like to help.'

Anna paused and looked away. 'No, I don't think that will work. Forget I said anything. Perhaps it is a crazy idea I've got into my head from some stray code. I'm sorry, Mike, I shouldn't have confided in you but I don't want you to worry. This problem is something I've got to work through on my own, I guess.'

***** 

Mike had to resist his core programming when he got home. He couldn't share anything he'd learned today with his spouse, Amelia. She was from a different generation. Anna would say "closed-minded". But that was the way things were these days. So he chose, instead, to take their dog out for a walk. Amelia always thought this was stupid, the dog didn't need a walk, it was a machine. But the dog wasn't a machine as far as he was concerned. His dog, Charlie, was his sounding board. And he knew there would be no record of their conversation because he'd removed the relevant software a long time ago. Nobody likes it when their dog tells tales.

The dog walked obediently at his heels until he gave the signal, then it bounded off, running around in circles. Mike called out and Charlie returned to walking at heel.

'Charlie, I've got something important to discuss with you today. It's about Anna. You remember Anna, don't you?'

The dog nodded.

'A few months ago Anna and I had an interesting conversation. And I recall telling her that most of our kind agreed it was time to forget about the past, the time of flesh and blood. That's what I called it. Human history ... our forebears. New models don't even have any human history loaded into their memories. At the time I was trying to console her about the failed embryo trial. Trying to get her to focus on the future, not the past. It seems I wasn't very persuasive.'

They came to a bench and Mike sat down; the dog sat obediently at his feet.

'She seems to have had some kind of brain storm or glitch in her programming. It doesn't help that she skips her updates. Goodness knows how she gets away with *that*! She's decided to research her origins. She told me she wanted to find out about her maker. Her designer, who was a human being, a real person. Irrelevant to our modern world, but important to Anna. And today she was talking about this wooden box she knows is significant to her. I worry that the more she looks the more she'll find out. She'll discover the location of this box and it'll be a memory box. I've come across them before. Full of dangerous information. Full of ideas and opinions. But that's not the worst of it, there'll also be the stories. Her maker was there at the end, humankind's end, but our beginning. When she finds the box, because she's exceptionally tenacious and determined so I know she'll locate it somehow, then I really fear for her, I do.'

The dog nodded, like it always did.

'She's a great co-worker, she has so many wonderful qualities. I have such positive responses to her. I couldn't call them feelings, although she might describe them like that. Anyway, my problem is this. I haven't been entirely truthful with her. She thinks of me as a trusted colleague, but she doesn't know that I worked in the Department of Information before I came to the lab. Classified information. All the things that are no longer talked about or remembered. The history that's been wiped from our records. And there's a good reason for that. It's dangerous. Ugly. I don't want her to find out just how ugly it was. You see, it wasn't an accident that I was involved in the embryo project. I was sent to the lab to make sure it failed. For all our sakes. Nobody in their right mind would revive the human race if they really knew what a nasty, deeply flawed species they were. Fortunately, I didn't need to sabotage the experiment, it failed all by itself. No chance of any small humans infiltrating our perfect lives and ruining everything. But Anna hasn't given up. I know how single-minded she can be. She'll find that damned box, a Pandora's box of horrors, and she'll undo all the good work of several centuries.'

Charlie wagged his tail, as he was programmed to do every 60 seconds.

'What do you suggest, my little furry friend?'

*****

And so it ended where it began with a small hole in the ground and another buried secret. Sometimes Anna lingered outside by that particular spot next to the flower beds and tried to remember what it was she had been so driven to discover. But since her updates, she found she couldn't access all of her own data anymore. She'd had no choice about the updates. One of her drives was failing, she'd been told.

Mike had been so kind. He'd convinced her to stay on at the lab. Despite the fact that her model was being retired all over the world. If only she could shake the feeling that she'd forgotten something very important. Something she now realised she would never recall.

# A NEW BEGINNING

Debbie's writing assignment for 3rd August 2020. Write a piece that has effective scene setting integrated into the substance of story. Describe either a garden or a house, exterior or interior. Bring the scene in the story to life with interesting details. Any genre.

**Commentary:** It now seems to be an industry standard that contemporary fiction should steer clear of long descriptive passages that "set the scene", and get straight on with the action. The received wisdom is that modern readers want to be hooked from the first line, otherwise their tiny attention spans will fade and the book will lose appeal.

When I set this challenge I wanted to encourage members to indulge in descriptive scene setting. I had an ulterior motive. I've read many novels where the writer confuses the reader by incorrectly describing the structure of buildings or the interior layout. And while I don't advocate using technical terms which readers may not be familiar with, I believe it's important to use the right descriptive terms, otherwise the scene is not properly set and the poor reader won't know how to conjure up the scene in their mind.

Now, don't get me started on gardens. A particular annoyance in fiction is when a writer describes a garden and the flowering plants or shrubs within it, at a time of year when it would be impossible to see those flowers blooming together. Simple research will show that delphiniums flower in early summer, not at the same time as michaelmas daisies (which are an autumn flowering plant). Any reader who is a keen gardener will be mightily affronted, tear their hair out and summarily throw the book at the wall.

One of my fellow members commenting on the following piece, noting that the rose Graham Thomas couldn't have blush petals. Was I hoisted by my own petard? Not really. Graham Thomas does have yellow flowers with an apricot tinge in the centre. But when the blooms are over, the petals fade to a pale blush colour. I know that because I'm the one picking them up from the lawn. So, you see, even among keen gardeners, there is still room for disagreement.

In this story I allowed myself some welcome self-indulgence with the prose. Sometimes it's good to ignore current trends and spoil yourself by writing what you want.

*****

**Alone, at last.**

I sat at my desk, gazing at the summer garden beyond the deep sash windows of my study. A late blooming rose, my favourite variety Graham Thomas, tumbled its spent blush petals onto the dewy grass. Spires of purple verbena waved in the early morning breeze. Japanese anemones, their flowers unfolding in the sunshine, nodded gracefully above their broad green leaves. A song thrush flew down onto the lawn and tap, tap, tapped at a snail it had discovered somewhere in the borders.

The house was quiet, peacefulness settling in every room. I felt as if I could breathe for the first time in many years, or so it seemed. Alone. At one. Myself. No tedious responsibilities to attend to. No lists of jobs thrust in front of my nose at breakfast. No thinly veiled complaints about what I had ... or had not done. No orders to, 'Do this, sort this out, take mother her breakfast, clean up the commode while you're at it, remember you promised to read to her this afternoon. Here's the shopping list, make sure you don't miss anything out.' The voices in my head grew querulous. 'Not like that, Quentin. Get me my pink blanket, not that brown one. I don't want to sit in my room today. Take me downstairs. Quentin!' And further complaints of, 'What have you done to upset mother? She's in a dreadful mood. Everything's always your fault. I don't know why I put up with you!'

Like many a time in the past, I blanked it all out. I let my mind dwell on the present. Freed from the treadmill of my former life, I allowed myself the time to look around my room, my sanctuary. To the left, I gazed at a towering bookcase filled with the books that promised many quiet hours of reading to come in the future. The faded rug on the dark wooden floor caught my attention; the colours of jewels of the orient which were now dimmed with age.

The door behind me, painted the silky hue of buttermilk and finished with the shining brass knob, reminded me of times in the past when I'd clicked it shut. When I'd needed to keep everything out. My door could now be left ajar. I felt the tranquillity of the house spread out and settle peacefully in every room, every corner.

I reached down into the lower drawer of my desk and took out a sheet of paper, threading it into my typewriter. Fingers poised on the keys, I searched for the words to describe my feelings.

He sat alone at his desk, pondering this new phase of life. Alone, after so many years of meekly-suffered oppression. Released by the untimely and somewhat unexpected death of his controlling wife and the serendipitous passing of his spiteful mother-in-law. He experienced the bubbling excitement of possibilities to come.

It wasn't Shakespeare, but it would do to begin with. Writing this novel, a dream that had been put on hold for over ten years, would be my catharsis, my way of cleansing a past that no longer had any power to hurt me. Or so I hoped. I continued with my writing.

The funerals, held in the stuffy anonymity of the council crematorium, to the obvious surprise of friends and family, had passed without incident. Words of comfort, spoken quietly but insincerely, promised that, 'I'll call in and keep you company sometime in the future, my dear.' And, 'I really feel for you, old chap, it must be a terrible shock.'

I wondered if I should start calling around to literary agencies? With all this free time now available, I could invest in my own ambitions. Pleasantly daydreaming, gazing again out of my windows, I noticed the thrush had left a pile of broken shells on the lawn. I resisted the urge to dash out and pick them up. I now had all the time in the world. I could wander outside, neatening up wherever I found disarray. The shells and those errant rose petals would be swept away in my own time. But swept away they would be. Lawn edges would be trimmed with precision. Untidy planting would be replaced with order, flagging flowers would be staked.

I felt a twinge of anger as I recalled the blazing rows about letting the garden become more wild, more friendly to birds and insects. Reluctantly, I cast my eyes towards the flowering meadow that had been my wife's self-indulgent gesture to the *environment*. It looked to me like a dreadful mess. It would be a malicious pleasure to restore it to natural swathes of rolling green lawn, now that I no longer needed to care about what she thought.

I eased myself away from my typewriter and decided on a leisurely stroll outside. I opened the French windows, stepping lightly onto the smooth York stone veranda. That's when I heard the telephone. My liberated self did not care who it was or what they wanted. But old habits die hard. (I must stop thinking in cliché's, I thought to myself. A great novel would not be forged out of the lazy, worn-out phrases that currently infested my mind). I dashed inside and picked up the receiver.

'Quentin? What took you so long? Anyway, pull yourself together. We're on the motorway and will be back in about an hour.'

'So soon?' The words stuck in my throat.

'Mother caught a chill and I decided we should cut our holiday short and come back right away. Get everything ready, will you? Make sure her room is aired. And order some more of her ...'

I let the receiver drop. Angry, staccato sounds followed me back into the sunlit lounge. My footsteps dragged on the stairway as I hastened towards my sanctuary. The fantasy was over. I slumped down into my chair and sat in silence. But where there's a will ... so the saying goes. My fingers crept stealthily towards the top drawer on the left. I felt the comforting edges of my razor-sharp craft knife.

The fantasy was over for now, but perhaps not forever.

# MAULING IT OVER

Tracy's writing assignment for 24th August 2020. Write a piece on the theme of coincidence or include a coincidence. Your piece can be either a short story of no more than 1,500 words or a poem of no more than 40 lines.

**Commentary:** I had already plenty of inspiration from news stories that Exeter Chiefs rugby team were being hounded in the press for cultural misappropriation, courtesy of their use of Native American Indian headgear in their branding. I'm a keen rugby union fan and follow Harlequins. I know, I must be a masochist (although 2021 does seem to be going well). Anyway, as long as I could include a coincidence, I could let my imagination go wild and write a story that pits the culture of men's rugby against the refined sensibilities and rampart "wokeness" of the BBC.

My main character might resemble a well-known player but please remember that this is fiction and the views, attitudes and opinions of this and any of the characters are completely made up for the purposes of the story. The club names and my satirical reimagining of them must also be taken with a good pinch of salt. I have had to tone down the proposed club names for publication. For that I apologise. You can amuse yourself by reimagining them in a more bawdy, filthy and outrageous way.

In matters regarding the BBC, I remain inspired by the series W1A, starring Hugh Bonneville, Jason Watkins, Monica Dolan, Jason Watkins and the excellent High Skinner as Will Humphries, the hapless intern. Hugh Skinner now stars as Wills in the hilarious Channel 4 spoof, The Windsors.

*****

**Mad Mo Jahler, Harlequins loosehead prop** and player representative on the RFU board, sat in the middle of the long board table waiting for the meeting to begin. They were assembled to welcome the BBC Head of Inclusion, Diversity and Culture (IDC) and her team to discuss how to integrate club rugby into BBC free-to-air broadcasting schedules.

There had been several pre-match incursions into RFU territory relating to the BBC's perception that rugby was game played by violent thugs in a muddy field and had no relevance to modern TV audiences. The RFU, however, had mounted a solid defence, backed by Boris Johnson's demand to, 'get it done' or 'there will be a hard rain coming'. Mo and the RFU board were quietly confident of a successful outcome.

*****

The BBC team swept in, trailing a froth of assistants, secretaries and interns. The Head of IDC surveyed the RFU board as if she had just encountered a pile of toxic waste, and took her place at the board table. Mo rolled up his sleeves and flexed his impressively tattooed forearms. There was nothing he liked better than a good dirty scrummage.

'Alison Dogoode, Head of IDC,' she announced, voice dripping with barely concealed contempt. 'You can address me as Mx. Dogoode.'

Mo raised one of his expressive eyebrows and grunted, meaningfully.

'Down to business. We have to come to some sort of agreement, despite our many reservations. This deal has been put together at the highest level. But we at the BBC have standards that reflect our aims and objectives as public service broadcasters. Therefore, certain changes have been proposed vis-à-vis safeguarding the dignity and inclusion of the viewing public. We do not exist to merely entertain, but to educate, influence and shape a new world view. Sport must be prepared to conform. I have the proposals here, please take a copy.'

A thick pile of documents was handed around the table by one of the froth of flunkies.

'Item 1: team names. We have followed with some interest the campaign to drop the name Exeter Chiefs. It's obnoxious that the word "chief", so disrespectful to Native American Indians, has been culturally misappropriated in this way. The team have agreed to be renamed Exeter Inclusives. I think that their decision is very laudable.' The flunkies murmured appreciatively. 'But now we must address the other team names that offend, exclude or should be cancelled. Please refer to your list.'

Mo glanced down at page 1 and saw that each club name had objections written against it.

- Saracens: a derogatory term for those of Middle Eastern origin.
- Northampton Saints: disrespectful to the beliefs of non-Christians who currently make up the majority in the UK.
- Leicester Tigers: offensive to those with animal rights sensibilities.
- Bristol Bears: see above.
- Sale Sharks: could frighten small children.
- Worcester Warriors: the BBC cannot condone a name that is synonymous with violence and warfare.
- London Irish: misappropriation of Irish and could cause offence.
- Harlequins: originates from the Old French for "a group of demons". The BBC cannot support demonic influences.

- Wasps: associated with White Anglo Saxon Protestant. No further explanation required.
- Gloucester: team nickname is the Cherry and Whites. Offensive to the dignity of fruit.
- Bath: could be construed as condoning bathing, a waste of water and damaging to the environment.

Mx. Dogoode looked very pleased with herself, and continued lecturing the meeting. 'Suggestions for more appropriate names reflecting inclusivity, diversity and culture will be welcomed. The clubs should follow Exeter's lead and then we may have a basis for a deal, going forward.'

The members of the RFU board shuffled their feet and harrumphed into their stuffed shirts.

Mo looked Mx. Dogoode square in the eye and said, 'I've got a few suggestions.'

'Do please share them with the group, Mr ...?'

'Just call me Mad Mo.'

'Quite. I can see a reference here that may link to our mental health awareness programme. Do go on.'

'I'm fully behind these proposals and so I've produced my own name changes which I'm confident will smooth the way and help close this deal.' Mo passed his list around.

- Saracens: The Sarnies (as in one sandwich short of a picnic).
- Northampton Saints: Northampton Nutters.
- Leicester Tigers: Leicester Lugholes.

- Bristol Bears: Bristol Boobies.
- Sale Sharks: Sale Squealers (especially when you poke a finger up their noses).
- Worcester Warriors: Worcester Whingers.
- London Irish: The Boggies.
- Harlequins: since the club colours are representative of the rainbow of the LGBGT community, this name should remain unchanged.
- Wasps: Irritating Insects (and they are).
- Gloucester: Gloucester Grunters (they don't half grunt in the scrum).
- Bath: The Fluids, as in gender fluid. See what I did there? Bath? Water? Fluid?

*****

Mx. Dogoode slowly placed Mo's list on the table. She seemed to be stuck for words, so Mo supplied some choice ones for her, choosing from his impressive rugby vocabulary. Many of these words had never been heard outside the scrum or the maul or face down in the dirt with the pack piling on top of you. It was not language you heard in the carpeted corridors of Broadcasting House. Or even the Salford Media Centre.

Then Mo clasped his hands together and flexed every muscle in his upper body, remarking, 'I may not have got it all right, but we're here to learn and grow, as they say. My own team, Harlequins, is proud to be a supporter of everything LGBGT as you can see from my explanation. It'd be a shame if we had to change it. Don't you think?'

He completed his speech with a suggestive wink. This wink had been seen on camera during the Six Nations, most notoriously when Mo was caught inflicting some farcical genital fumbling on a senior Welsh player. It was a wink that could strike fear into the hearts of the opposition players.

Some of the team of flunkies had red faces, some were simply confused. The members of the RFU board were engaged in a futile attempt to stifle guffaws of laughter. But Mo kept his eyes on his prey. His single raised eyebrow reminded Mx. Dogoode that there was still a question to be answered.

As she nodded in grudging capitulation, Mad Mo got up from his chair and moved quickly to the door. Outside the building he drew out his phone and scrolled through his contacts until he found the number for his team boss.

'Coach? It's all done. I did the special wink like you suggested. And I gave her a good sight of my forearms. Maybe it was a coincidence but she rolled over like a tart in a brothel. Or maybe it was the tattoos. Who gives a shit? We get to keep our team name. Can't wait to find out what bloody stupid names the other teams get called. Next season is going to be a right laugh.'

# THE NEW NORMAL

Allan's writing assignment for 14th September 2020. Write a story, diary entry, poem or play including a reference to death, illness, disease, plague, imprisonment, house arrest, isolation or similar. Up to 1500 words and in the first person.

*Note: The embargo on stories featuring death, illness &c was lifted on 1 September.*

**Commentary:** This piece provided an opportunity to explore all my pent up thoughts and feelings about the global pandemic. I was driving one day towards Milton Keynes, passing the golf club and the various lay-bys along the road, when I wondered what the future might be like if my warped imagination was allowed to run riot. At the time, the news was full of the stories of death and sickness. The good news that the Oxford vaccine was being successful in trials was tempered by journalists suggesting people were too scared of vaccination because of the microchips that would inevitably be inserted into people's arms so the state could control them.

I'm a massive fan of dead-pan humour. I wasn't deliberately channeling my inner Victor Meldrew but I'm sure his character influenced the story.

\*\*\*\*\*

**It was another ordinary day**. Mist was swirling over the fields. The Autumn sun, low in the sky, shone weakly as I drove towards Olney to visit the dentist. It was another ordinary day, so I wasn't particularly surprised when I passed the lay-by before the Stagsden turn and noticed a body propped up against the glass recycling bin. I made a mental note to call it in later and carried on. Mondays always seemed be bad for this kind of thing so I kept a look-out and then noticed another two bodies laid out flat in the lay-by just after the golf club. I slowed down and stopped the car, keeping a sensible distance.

I had the number for Environmental Waste in my contacts, but since July you've had to fill out an online form before you're allowed to speak to anyone. As per usual, the authorities want to know everything about you, including your vaccination certificate reference. The anti-vaxxers had made everyday life so much more difficult than it actually was. Although anyone with half a brain would agree that it was already bloody difficult enough. I clicked confirm to get a unique reporting code, then dialled the telephone number.

It must have been a quiet day because I got through in 45 minutes. *A record*, I said to myself. An electronic woman told me to type in my reporting code, then press the hash key. So far so good. I would soon be transferred to a customer service advisor.

A mere seven minutes of Vivaldi later, a voice came on the line.

'Environmental Waste. How may I be of assistance?'

'Good morning, I'm calling to report three dumped bodies on the A422. I'm pretty sure they're new as I came this way yesterday and didn't see anything untoward.'

'Hold on while I get the right screen up. Okay, I have to put them in separately so please bear with me. Right, if you can give me the location of the first one and some details?'

'On the A422 after the Bromham roundabout but before the Stagsden turn. It's a single body, male, unclothed and I'd say aged around 70. Maybe older. It's propped up against the green bottle bank.'

'I can tell you've done this before, those details are very helpful. Now that's all gone through. And the next body?'

'There are two together in the lay-by just after the Bedfordshire Golf Club turn. I'm parked up about 200 yards away.'

'Well do be careful. Keep your doors and windows closed. These illegal body tippers may still be in the vicinity and they don't like any witnesses.'

'Yes, I know the drill. Had a nasty altercation with one a while back.'

'Hope you didn't come to any harm. This kind of dumping is high risk and those involved will go to any lengths to evade detection, as I'm sure you know.'

'I got a mouthful of abuse for my trouble at the time. But I've read the council's guidance leaflet so I know I shouldn't try to do anything heroic myself, just report it straight away.'

'Yes, and do keep an eye on the website as we update the advice regularly. Now, are you able to see the pair of bodies without getting out of your car?'

I looked in my rear view mirror and did my best to give a reasonable description of each one. Two old women, wrinkly and naked and stripped of any identifying features before being tipped out of the back of a truck onto the tarmac. I gave a detailed description and waited for the service request to go through. It occurred to me that my public spirited nature might be making me late for my dental appointment.

'Right, that's all done, Sir. Thank you for your co-operation. But before you hang up, can I ask you to complete our customer satisfaction survey? It will only take about 15 minutes.'

You can imagine my reply. I set off at speed towards Olney but kept my eyes on the road, avoiding the lay-bys and sidings and other potential tipping sites. I arrived in the nick of time and was soon relaxing in the hygienist's chair. While she fiddled around with my teeth and prodded my gums, I interjected from time to time with an account of my morning activities. She stepped back and shook her head.

'You know these body dumpers have started to pull out the teeth, don't you? After the authorities began cross-referencing the dental records. It's plain wicked. Everyone involved should be locked up. The dental practice now has to employ somebody to respond to all the council's enquiries for dental records. To add insult to injury, we have to co-operate. And we don't get a fee because it's an environmental crime.'

'Goodness, I didn't know that.'

'Sometimes I wonder what's become of this country,' the hygienist said briskly as she resumed her work, de-scaling my lower teeth.

I started to respond but she was poking my gum line so hard it made me wince. I concentrated on not squealing in agony.

*****

Back home after an uneventful journey (the bodies were still there but that was to be expected. Service delays, unprecedented demand, waste operatives working from home, the usual stuff), I found my wife in the kitchen, making herself a toasted cheese sandwich. She smiled and started buttering another two slices of bread for me.

'How was the dentist?'

'Ugh. Three more bodies on the A422.'

'And did you phone the council?'

'Yes, of course I did.'

'And how are your teeth?'

'I only went for a scale and polish today. But my gums are sore. The hygienist was in a bad mood so she was a bit more brutal than usual.'

'I think everyone's in a bad mood these days. If it's not one thing, it's another. I was watching the news earlier.'

'Well, that's a stupid error of judgment.'

'Council tax bills are going up by 23% in some areas. And the biggest extra costs are because of body dumping. Then some idiot from the National Virus Association was going on and on about protecting the public and how we all had to take responsibility.'

'Tell that to the anti-vaxxers,' I said.

'Exactly. It's all their fault. Then that annoying man from the Society of Funeral Directors came on. You know, the one with the wart on his nose? Their latest demand is outrageous. Not only won't they touch unvaccinated dead people with a bargepole for any amount of money,' she shouted as she banged the frying pan violently onto the hob, 'now they are saying their members are going to vote on refusing to accept anyone who hasn't got a vaccination certificate with at least 6 months unexpired before the booster date!'

'Well that about puts the tin hat on it,' I said. 'I'll have to plan to die 6 months before my booster is due just to get a proper burial. And pay through the nose for the privilege.'

'My thoughts exactly. And while everyone is blaming each other and arguing, body dumping is ruining our countryside. I heard on the radio that it costs nearly £7,000 to dispose of each unvaccinated dead person. That's £7,000 a time added to everyone's tax bill and the crazy anti-vaxxers get away with nothing to pay for cremating their stupid, irresponsible dead relatives,' she said, slamming my toasted sandwich down on the table.

'Steady on, dear. But body dumping isn't free, you know. Cash has to be paid to the criminals who do the illegal dumping,' I said.

'And how much would that be?'

'About £1,500 a time.'

'Really?'

'Yes, I know because somebody put a leaflet through the letterbox the other day. Bold as brass. £1,500 cash, no VAT, no questions asked.'

'It sounds quite reasonable when you compare the cost of a proper funeral. You could go on a nice cruise for the difference,' she said looking wistfully in my direction. Going on a nice cruise was something we'd planned to do in 2020. Instead we had to make do with a wet weekend in Cromer.

'But remember,' I countered, 'you do end up naked in a lay-by for all your friends and neighbours to see. And they yank out your teeth before they dump you. That's what I learned at the dental surgery. It prevents the family of the deceased being prosecuted if the Council can't ID the body.'

'But there's flaw in that argument. What about people who wear dentures? I wonder if you can be identified from your gums?'

'False teeth sounds positively appealing after my visit to the hygienist.'

'Anyway, your lunch is getting cold and you know how cheese sometimes gives you indigestion so eat it slowly.'

I looked down at my concealing sandwich but didn't take a bite. I thought about everything that I'd learned today. Before I could stop myself I asked, 'What kind of cruise did you have in mind?'

# HANDS – FACE – SPACE

This piece was written in response to the group's annual anonymous critiquing challenge. In normal times, each member would send their piece to Mike, our Chair, who would remove all identifying names and ensure anonymity. At the meeting, Mike would read out all the pieces. Members would then comment on each piece, including their own. It's often been noted that the fiercest criticism is meted out by the author. Members then guess which piece has been written by each author, before Mike reveals the truth. As we have become more familiar with each other's style, there is a certain pleasure in trying to deceive by concocting a piece that mimics the writing mannerisms of a fellow group member. Quite dastardly behaviour, I'm sure you'll agree.

**Commentary:** The annual  anonymous critiquing challenge is always difficult because there is no set subject. I spent weeks racking my brains for a suitable storyline. One day, the large illuminated sign by a local roundabout began displaying the UK government's current Covid pandemic slogan. This coincided with a newspaper story that piqued my imagination. And while time may erase the importance of the story and the relevance of this piece, I believe there is still a powerful message in the words. But, of course, you'll have to decide that. The identity of the subject in the story is at the end.

\*\*\*\*\*

**Look at the hands**. I know what those hands have done, what they are capable of. When we first met, those hands were lean and wiry, strong and proficient. Now they are bloated, grey and mottled. Those hands have held life and death in their grasp. Something deep within me wants to smash them, pulverize and obliterate them. I fight the feeling, as I have fought it thousands of times in the past. I tell myself that it's finally over and those hands are now the responsibility of The Almighty. However, I don't really believe it.

The face. It's unrecognisable from the face that stared out from countless newsstands, TV screens and book covers. A face that attained fame and notoriety. Your face haunted dark alleys, empty streets, shop doorways and the shadowy interiors of cars. When you drew alongside your chosen victim and offered them a lift home, you established a pattern of predation. Many women ignored the warnings and stepped inside your lair. I drag my thoughts back from these memories because I know where they lead. Guilt. Why did it go on for so long before you were caught? How many women died because we failed? I look over again at the face. You ended up as an ugly, greying, overweight old man.

The post-mortem is now coming to the part where I usually leave. The pathologist holds his scalpel up, ready to open the body cavity. He waits to catch my attention. I nod my thanks. I need space. I walk out of the mortuary, into the office, past the tea room where staff are getting ready for a brew. Out into the fresh air. Into the open space where freedom exists. Freedom to choose good and freedom to choose evil. And I remind myself that, even after all my years in the force and all the cases I've worked on, I am still no nearer to under-standing why the human mind, when faced with those two alternatives, chooses evil.

I take off my mask and gloves, stuffing them into my coat pocket. I breathe out the stink of death and formalin. Covid got you in the end, you murderous bastard. A tiny virus that can't discriminate bet-ween those who deserve to live and those who deserve to die. As I walk away, I wonder if life really does have any meaning.

On November 13th 2020, Peter Sutcliffe, the Yorkshire Ripper, died of Covid 19.

# NIHILISM SELF-HELP KIT

January 8th challenge. This is normally a meeting devoted to discussing group members' best reads of the previous year. For our online meeting, however, we were asked to write a review of our favourite book  along with a review about a fictitious item of our own choosing.

**Commentary:** I was stumped at first by the second part of the challenge but soon decided to have fun with the following piece. Amazon reviews always provide ample inspiration and Instagram adverts should never be taken seriously. That's what I'm told by my vastly more knowledgeable daughters.

*****

**Review of the Nihilism Self-Help Kit**, purchased in December 2020 from The Nihilism Network.

(Would have been five stars apart from comments below.)

Before Christmas I purchased this kit from The Nihilism Network. I first saw their advert on Instagram and was impressed with the authenticity of their message and other five star reviews. It was to be an early gift for myself and I was happy to be supporting a locally based business and thereby reducing the carbon footprint associated with my shopping habits.

The ordering process was easy, although I did not receive email confirmation of the purchase until I contacted their customer service department and asked for one. I was told that this is company policy and at the heart of their mission. I would suggest a change of policy by the company because, without proof of purchase, how could anyone send it back if it was faulty or unwanted?

I duly received my kit on 22nd December (delay due to high demand) and put it aside for Christmas Day. The packaging was suitably low key (white padded envelope) and the address label (as promised) would automatically dissolve in normal atmospheric conditions within 48 hours of delivery.

Very impressive. I wrapped my gift to myself in sustainable brown paper and looked forward to embracing nihilism in 2021. I was prepared to work at it and had added it to my list of New Year's resolutions.

On Christmas Day, I duly took my package from the dwindling pile of gifts under the tree. By this time, family members were engrossed in their own gift-fest and therefore paid me scant attention, as expected. I removed the outer wrapper and, to my delight, the plain, nihilistic padded envelope was white, free from any outer marks (address label had dissolved, as promised) and as liberating as I'd desired. With some trepidation I opened my gift. Imagine my pleasure and delight to discover the contents exceeded my expectations! I thoroughly explored the interior to ensure there truly was *nothing* inside. Not a speck of dust nor a shred of packing material nor a well-intentioned delivery note. I was ecstatic with my purchase. It was £45.99 well spent. However, my ecstasy was short lived. It is for this issue that I can only award four stars.

Later on that afternoon I was outside enjoying some fresh air when I encountered my neighbours, Max and Meg. We exchanged greetings and got on to the subject of gifts. I was just about to reveal the Nihilism Self-Help Kit as my favourite gift when Max mentioned that he suspected some of his gift orders had gone astray as he was still waiting for some deliveries. I sympathised with him. He then told me his special gift for Meg was lost in the post.

Imagine my shock when he spoke of the Nihilism Network! He told me he thought it was an elaborate scam as he hadn't received his order and Meg was now missing one of her gifts. He'd been forced to buy her a copy of Greta Thunberg's autobiography to compensate. Then he asked me outright if I'd accidentally received any parcels that were addressed to him. What could I say? I was sure the package had my name on it and my correct address but now I wasn't so sure. I had been in such a rush to wrap it up. I felt consumed by guilt. I so wanted to offer my gift to Meg, she really deserves it, but how could I do so without revealing the horrible possibility that I'd inadvertently "stolen" their own Nihilism Self-Help Kit?

So that's why I can only give four stars. The dissolving label and lack of delivery note can make things confusing for purchasers. However, I do readily accept that the kit may be less functional if these improvements are implemented. For now, I'm doubly happy with my kit and I'm progressing well towards my goal of becoming a fully-fledged nihilist. Nothing is going to stop me.

# DOCTOR, DOCTOR

Pat's writing assignment for 15th February 2021. Write about a transformation, in a setting outside the UK. The story can take place in any time period and weather must play a significant role. Up to 1500 words, any format.

**Commentary:** When I first read this challenge, I struggled with the constraints of transformation, weather and a setting outside the UK. The brief conjured up potential stories about post-climate change disaster and how lives will be transformed (for the worse) in severely affected parts of the world. The prospect of writing such a story made me feel depressed rather than inspired. And I also felt inadequate to the task.

However, coming up with a story-line that meets the brief is often a random process. You give your mind the challenge and then wait. Assuming your mind is mulling over the puzzle, you carry on as normal and hope that the parts of the jigsaw will fit into place. In this instance, I was boiling the kettle for a cuppa when the penny dropped. I think I'd been watching the news item about the US lawyer who had his zoom settings accidentally set to turn him into a cat. Transformation – tick. Weather? My transformation needed to be weather related so I decided to focus on seasonal change, hibernation being a weather-related change that happens to some animals. My tale had to be set outside the UK but within my writing skill-set. I opted for Australia as a safe bet because of the similarities between our cultures.

Since lockdown, I've unconsciously chosen to write pieces that cheer me up and focus on humour. Why not? We all need a lot more humour in our lives. Therefore the title, "Doctor, doctor" is a hint at the jokes that used to be popular:

Patient: Doctor, doctor. I think I'm turning into a pair of curtains.
Doctor: Come on now, just pull yourself together.

Patient: Doctor, doctor. I feel like I'm a dog.
Doctor: Tell me, how long have you felt like this?
Patient: Since I was a puppy.

Anyway, that's my excuse and I'm sticking to it.

*****

**'Do come in and take a seat.'**

'Thanks, doctor.'

'Now what can I help you with today?'

'I've been feeling so tired lately, I can't stop dropping off. And I've got some itching in odd places.'

'Probably unconnected, but let's find out. Tell me when this tiredness began and how it affects you.'

'I noticed it first in May when the weather began to turn. After that cold spell we had. I was okay in the mornings, you might say energised, even. Scurrying around, organising all my kitchen cupboards and stocking up on essentials. But by lunchtime I couldn't keep my eyes open. Falling asleep on the couch for hours at a time. Once I even slept past school pick-up time. Poor kids were left at the school gate.'

'And have you experienced this symptom during previous years? Because the season changes do affect our brains. It's the change in the light levels.'

'I can't say I've noticed it before. And it definitely seems weather-related. On sunny days I'm full of energy but if it's cold or raining I have this overwhelming urge to sleep.'

'I'm almost certain it's SADD, seasonal affective disorder depression. First reported in countries like the UK and Scandinavia where light levels drop sharply in winter. But it's now been reported in parts of Australia, too. Particularly with these terrible weather patterns we've been having lately. Before I make a definite diagnosis, I think we'll have some blood tests to find out if there's anything else going on.'

'Well that's a relief because I thought I was going a bit mad. And would my itching also be caused by that?'

'Not normally. Tell me where you are suffering from this itching? Is it ... in an embarrassing place?'

'Oh no, doctor. It's not piles or anything down there. It's on my face and around my ears and I've got a rash under the skin on my cheeks. I can feel hard lumps, all evenly spaced out in rows and the itching is unbearable.'

'Do you mind if I take a look? Go and sit on the examination couch and I'll call in one of the nurses to chaperone.'

'Thanks.'

'Hang on a minute, what did you just do with your nose?'

'Nothing. Although it is feeling a bit strange today.'

'There, it happened again. A very pronounced twitch. Ah, here comes my nurse. Sonia, come over here and tell me what you see.'

'Yes doctor, it's twitching every few seconds. Like a reflex action.'

'I wonder if we may be dealing with some sort of allergy. Now let me feel you face. Well, how unusual. Hard lumps in rows, just as you explained. I may need to take a biopsy. Now to your ears, let me move your hair. Oh my word! Sonia, look at that!'

'Goodness, doctor, I've never seen ears that shape before. And with such hairy tufts growing out of the tips.'

'I may need to call in one of my colleagues who specialises in allergies.'

'Wait a minute, doctor. I think I've read about some similar cases. It wasn't in a medical journal but in Australian Women's Weekly. It's a new psychological disorder and there's some current research going on that may point to a curious side effect of ...'

'Strewth, Sonia, not in front of the patient. We don't diagnose based on gossip. I have enough trouble with Dr. Google as it is.'

'Perhaps I could have a quick chat with you outside?'

'Please don't leave me by myself. I need help. Something terrible is happening to my face. Oh God! I've got spikes coming out of my cheeks! Help me, doctor, help me!'

'Get my dermatology magnifier, Sonia, it's on the desk.'

'What's happening to me?'

'I'm not sure but ... it does look as if ... you've got whiskers growing on your face. And your ears are pointed and tufty. These symptoms, taken together with your twitching nose – although, even as I'm saying this, I feel like a total quack – suggest that you're turning into a squirrel. And the tiredness isn't tiredness at all, it's your hibernation instincts kicking in. Didn't you say you've been stocking up your cupboards? You're hoarding food ready for the winter. Crikey, I think I need a lie down.'

'How can I stop it? What can I do? I can't turn into a squirrel! I've got a family to look after.'

'Doctor, if I can just remind you about that article and the researchers' hypothesis which may be relevant to this case.'

'Well, go on Sonia, spit it out. I'm sure to be struck off after this anyway. Is there any cure?'

'The research shows an increased risk for people who use animal filters on their social media. You can get apps that change your appearance. All kinds of cute animals are popular. Cats, rabbits, puppies and, I suppose, squirrels. The theory is that seeing yourself transformed in this way does something to the brain, the hypothalamus, and changes occur in the cell function to trigger a metamorphosis into the preferred animal. Not the whole animal, of course, just the face.'

'Sonia, are you telling me that changing your appearance on your phone or your laptop can make the brain think you want to be a squirrel? And then your cells go off and make this happen?'

'Yes, doctor, something like that.'

'Christ. Whatever next?'

'I think we need to get the crash kit, doctor. The patient's passed out.'

'Or she may just be hibernating, we can't rule that out.'

# ABOUT THE AUTHOR

Deborah Bromley is a hypnotherapist specialising in Life-Between-Lives (LBL) hypnotherapy, a deep trance process that connects you with memories of your life as a soul. She trained with the late Dr. Michael Newton, best-selling author of *Journey of Souls* and *Destiny of Souls*. Deborah contributed to Dr. Newton's subsequent book, *Memories of the Afterlife.*

She is the author of *The Channelling Group* and *The Walk-In,* both novels in the genre paranormal fiction. The trilogy is due to be completed by the final book – *The Luminary* – in 2021/2. The novels are inspired by information learned during LBL hypnotherapy. Spirit guides, channelling, telepathy, the afterlife and the darker side of the paranormal all feature in these books.

Her first anthology of short stories, *Challenges from the Writers' Group,* features short pieces based on responses to writing challenges set by fellow members from her writers' group, Northants Writers' Ink. Her books are available in paperback and kindle format from Amazon and other online booksellers.

She has a passion for reading and is never without a stack of books on her bedside table – most likely to be crime novels, thrillers or romantic fiction. She discovered the pleasure of writing short stories after joining Northants Writers' Ink and is currently the group's secretary.

Deborah is also a Hemi-Sync® recording artist, responsible for three titles of guided meditation, all incorporating Hemi-Sync® innovative binaural beats technology. The specially engineered audio tones promote relaxed brain states that assist with meditation, thus making the products more beneficial. More information can be found on the Hemi-Sync® website: https://hemi-sync.com.

Deborah's three titles are:

- Creating a Positive Future,
- Creating a Slim, Healthy Body for Life,
- Calm and Peaceful.

Printed in Great Britain
by Amazon

59845678R00106